Jarwin and

R.M. Ballantyne

Alpha Editions

ISBN : 9789353297077

Design and Setting By
Alpha Editions
email - alphaedis@gmail.com

Contents

Chapter One

Adrift on the Ocean

On a certain morning, not very long ago, the sun, according to his ancient and admirable custom, rose at a very early hour, and casting his bright beams far and wide over the Pacific, lighted up the yellow sands and the verdant hills of one of the loveliest of the islands of that mighty sea.

It was early morning, as we have said, and there was plenty of life—animal as well as vegetable—to be seen on land and sea, and in the warm, hazy atmosphere. But there were no indications of man's presence in that beautiful scene. The air was perfectly calm, yet the gentle swell of the ocean terminated in great waves, which came rolling in like walls of glass, and fell on the coral-reef like rushing snow-wreaths with a roar as loud as thunder.

Thousands of sea-birds screamed and circled in the sky. Fish leaped high out of their native element into the air, as if they wished to catch the gulls, while the gulls, seemingly smitten with a similar desire, dived into the water as if they wished to catch the fish. It might have been observed, however, that while the fish never succeeded in catching the gulls, the latter very frequently caught the fish, and, without taking the trouble to kill them, bolted them down alive.

Cocoanut-palms cast the shadows of their long stems and graceful tops upon the beach, while, farther inland, a dense forest of tropical plants—bread-fruit trees, bananas, etcetera—rose up the mountain-sides. Here and there open patches might be seen, that looked like fields and lawns, but there were no cottages or villas. Droves of pigs rambled about the valleys and on the hill-sides, but they were wild pigs. No man tended them. The bread-fruits, the cocoanuts, the bananas, the plantains, the plums, all were beautiful and fit for food, but no man owned them or used them, for, like many other spots in that sea of coral isles and savage men, the island was uninhabited.

In all the wide expanse of ocean that surrounded that island, there was nothing visible save one small, solitary speck on the far-off horizon. It might have been mistaken for a seagull, but it was in reality a raft—a mass of spars and planks rudely bound together with ropes. A boat's mast rose from the centre of it, on which hung a rag of sail, and a small red flag drooped motionless from its summit. There were a few casks on the highest part of the raft, but no living soul was visible. Nevertheless, it was not without tenants. In a hollow between two of the spars, under the shadow of one of the casks, lay the form of a man. The canvas trousers, cotton shirt, blue jacket, and open necktie, bespoke him a sailor, but it seemed as though there were nothing left save the dead body of the unfortunate tar, so pale and thin and ghastly were his features. A terrier dog lay beside him, so shrunken that it looked like a mere scrap of door-matting. Both man and dog were apparently dead, but they were not so in reality, for, after lying about an hour quite motionless, the man slowly opened his eyes.

Ah, reader, it would have touched your heart to have seen those eyes! They were so deep set, as if in dark caverns, and so unnaturally large. They gazed round in a vacant way for a few moments, until they fell on the dog. Then a gleam of fire shot through them, and their owner raised his large, gaunt, wasted frame on one elbow, while he gazed with a look of eagerness, which was perfectly awful, at his dumb companion.

"Not dead *yet!*" he said, drawing a long sigh.

There was a strange, incongruous mixture of satisfaction and discontent in the remark, which was muttered in a faint whisper.

Another gleam shot through the large eyes. It was not a pleasant look. Slowly, and as if with difficulty, the man drew a clasp-knife from his pocket, and opened it. As he did so, his brows lowered and his teeth became clenched. It was quite plain what he meant to do. As he held the open knife over the dog's head, he muttered, "Am I to die for the sake of a *dog!*"

Either the terrier's slumbers had come to an end naturally, at a fortunate moment, or the master's voice had awakened it, for it opened its eyes, raised its head, and looked up in the sailor's face. The hand with the knife drooped a little. The dog rose and licked it. Hunger had done its work on the poor creature, for it could hardly stand, yet it managed to look in its master's face with that grave, simple gaze of self-forgetting love, which appears to be peculiar to the canine race. The savage glare of the seaman's eyes vanished. He dropped the knife.

"Thanks, Cuffy; thanks for stoppin' me. It would have been *murder*! No, no, my doggie, you and I shall die together."

His voice sank into a murmur, partly from weakness and partly from the ideas suggested by his concluding words.

"Die together!" he repeated, "surely it ain't come to that *yet*. Wot, John Jarwin, you're not goin' to give in like that, are you? to haul down your colours on a fine day with a clear sky like this overhead? Come, cheer up, lad; you're young and can hold out a good while yet. Hey, old dog, wot say *you*?"

The dog made a motion that would, in ordinary circumstances, have resulted in the wagging of its tail, but the tail was powerless to respond.

At that moment a gull flew towards the raft; Jarwin watched it eagerly as it approached. "Ah," he muttered, clasping his bony hand as tightly over his heart as his strength would allow and addressing the gull, "if I only had hold of *you*, I'd tear you limb from limb, and drink your blood!"

He watched the bird intently as it flew straight over him. Leaning back, he continued slowly to follow its flight, until his head rested on the block of wood which had served him for a pillow. The support felt agreeable, he forgot the gull, closed his eyes, and sank with a deep sigh into a slumber that strongly resembled death.

Presently he awoke with a start, and, once more raising himself, gazed round upon the sea. No ship was to be seen. How often he had gazed round the watery circle with the same anxious look only to meet with disappointment! The hills of the coral island were visible like a blue cloud on the horizon, but Jarwin's eyes were too dim and worn out to observe them.

"Come," he exclaimed, suddenly, scrambling to his feet, "rouse up, Cuffy; you an' I ain't a-goin' to die without a good fight for life. Come along, my hearty; we'll have another glass of grog—Adam's grog it is, but it has been good grog to you an' me, doggie—an' then we shall have another inspection o' the locker; mayhap there's the half of a crumb left."

The comparatively cheery tone in which the sailor said this seemed to invigorate the dog, for it rose and actually succeeded in wriggling its tail as it staggered after its master—indubitable sign of hope and love not yet subdued!

Jarwin went to a cask which still contained a small quantity of fresh water. Three weeks before the point at which we take up his story, a storm had left him and his dog the sole survivors on the raft of the crew of a barque which had sprung a leak, and gone to the bottom. His provision at the time was a very small quantity of biscuit and a cask of fresh water. Several days before this the last biscuit had been consumed but the water had not yet failed. Hitherto John Jarwin had husbanded his provisions, but now, feeling desperate, he drank deeply of the few remaining drops of that liquid which, at the time, was almost as vital to him as his life-blood. He gave a full draught also to the little dog.

"Share and share alike, doggie," he said, patting its head, as it eagerly lapped up the water; "but there's no wittles, Cuffy, an' ye don't care for baccy, or ye should be heartily welcome to a quid."

So saying, the sailor supplied his own cheek with a small piece of his favourite weed, and stood up on the highest part of the raft to survey the surrounding prospect. He did so without much hope, for "hope deferred" had at last made his heart sick. Suddenly his wandering gaze became fixed and intense. He shaded his eyes with one hand, and steadied himself against the mast with the other. There could be no doubt of it! "Land ho!" he shouted, with a degree of strength that surprised himself, and even drew from Cuffy the ghost of a bark. On the strength of the discovery Jarwin and his dumb friend immediately treated themselves to another glass of Adam's grog.

But poor Jarwin had his patience further tried. Hours passed away, and still the island seemed as far off as ever. Night drew on, and it gradually faded from his view. But he had unquestionably seen land; so, with this to comfort him, the starving tar lay down beside his dog to spend another night—as he had already spent many days and nights—a castaway on the wide ocean.

Morning dawned, and the sailor rose with difficulty. He had forgotten, for a moment, the discovery of land on the previous night, but it was brought suddenly to his remembrance by the roar of breakers near at hand. Turning in the direction whence the sound came, he beheld an island quite close to him, with heavy "rollers" breaking furiously on the encircling ring of the coral-reef. The still water between the reef and the shore, which was about a quarter of a mile wide, reflected every tree and crag of the island, as if in a mirror. It was a grand, a glorious sight, and caused Jarwin's heart to swell with emotions that he had never felt before; but his attention was quickly turned to a danger which was imminent, and which seemed to threaten the total destruction of his raft, and the loss of his life.

A very slight breeze—a mere zephyr—which had carried him during the night towards the island, was now bearing him straight, though slowly, down on the reef, where, if he had once got involved in the breakers, the raft must certainly have been dashed to pieces; and he knew full well, that in his weak condition, he was utterly incapable of contending with such a surf.

Being a man of promptitude, his first act, on making this discovery, was to lower the sail. This was, fortunately, done in time; had he kept it up a few minutes longer, he must inevitably have passed the only opening in the reef that existed on that side of the island. This opening was not more than fifty yards wide. To the right and left of it the breakers on the reef extended, in lines of seething foam. Already the raft was rolling in the commotion caused by these breakers, as it drifted towards the opening.

Jarwin was by no means devoid of courage. Many a time, in days gone by, when his good ship was tossing on the stormy sea, or scudding under bare poles, had he stood on the deck with unshaken confidence and a calm heart, but now he was face to face with the seaman's most dreaded enemy—"breakers ahead!"—nay, worse, breakers around him everywhere, save at that one narrow passage, which appeared so small, and so involved in the general turmoil, as to afford scarcely an element of hope. For the first time in his life Jarwin's heart sank within him—at least so he said in after years while talking of the event—but we suspect that John was underrating himself. At all events, he showed no symptoms of fear as he sat there calmly awaiting his fate.

As the raft approached the reef, each successive roller lifted it up and dropped it behind more violently, until at last the top of one of the glittering green walls broke just as it passed under the end of the raft nearest the shore. Jarwin now knew that the next billow would seal his fate.

There was a wide space between each of those mighty waves. He looked out to sea, and beheld the swell rising and taking form, and increasing in speed as it came on. Calmly divesting himself of his coat and boots, he sat down beside his dog, and awaited the event. At that moment he observed, with intense gratitude to the Almighty, that the raft was drifting so straight towards the middle of the channel in the reef, that there seemed every probability of being carried through it; but the hope thus raised was somewhat chilled by the feeling of weakness which pervaded his frame.

"Now, Cuffy," said he, patting the terrier gently, "rouse up, my doggie; we must make a brave struggle for life. It's neck or nothing this time. If we touch that reef in passing, Cuff, you an' I shall be food for the sharks to-night, an' it's my opinion that the shark as gits us won't have much occasion to boast of his supper."

The sailor ceased speaking abruptly. As he looked back at the approaching roller he felt solemnised and somewhat alarmed, for it appeared so perpendicular and so high from his low position, that it seemed as if it would fall on and overwhelm the raft. There was, indeed, some danger of this. Glancing along its length, Jarwin saw that here and there the edge was lipping over, while in one place, not far off, the thunder of its fall had already begun. Another moment, and it appeared to hang over his head; the raft was violently lifted at the stern, caught up, and whirled onward at railway speed, like a cork in the midst of a boiling cauldron of foam. The roar was deafening. The tumultuous heaving almost overturned it several times. Jarwin held on firmly to the mast with his right arm, and grasped the terrier with his left hand, for the poor creature had not strength to resist such furious motion. It all passed with bewildering speed. It seemed as if, in one instant, the raft was hurled through the narrows, and launched into the calm harbour within. An eddy, at the inner side of the opening, swept it round, and fixed the end of one of the largest spars of which it was composed on the beach.

There were fifty yards or so of sandy coral-reef between the beach outside, that faced the sea, and the beach inside, which faced the land; yet how great the difference! The one beach, buffeted for ever, day and night, by the breakers—in calm by the grand successive rollers that, as it were, symbolised the ocean's latent power—in storm by the mad deluge of billows which displayed that power in all its terrible grandeur. The other beach, a smooth, sloping circlet of fair white sand, laved only by the ripples of the lagoon, or by its tiny wavelets, when a gale chanced to sweep over it from the land.

Jarwin soon gained this latter beach with Cuffy in his arms, and sat down to rest, for his strength had been so much reduced that the mere excitement of passing through the reef had almost exhausted him. Cuffy, however, seemed to derive new life from the touch of earth again, for it ran about in a staggering drunken sort of way; wagged its tail at the root,—without, however, being able to influence the point,—and made numerous futile efforts to bark.

In the midst of its weakly gambols the terrier chanced to discover a dead fish on the sands. Instantly it darted forward and began to devour it with great voracity.

"Halo! Cuffy," shouted Jarwin, who observed him; "ho! hold on, you rascal! share and share alike, you know. Here, fetch it here!"

Cuffy had learned the first great principle of a good and useful life—whether of man or beast—namely, prompt obedience. That meek but jovial little dog, on receiving this order, restrained its appetite, lifted the fish in its longing jaws, and, carrying it to his master, humbly laid it at his feet. He was rewarded with a hearty pat on the head, and a full half of the coveted fish—for Jarwin appeared to regard the "share-and-share-alike" principle as a point of honour between them.

The fish was not good, neither was it large, and of course it was raw, besides being somewhat decayed; nevertheless, both man and dog ate it, bones and all, with quiet satisfaction. Nay, reader, do not shudder! If you were reduced to similar straits, you would certainly enjoy, with equal gusto, a similar meal, supposing that you had the good fortune to get it. Small though it was, it sufficed to appease the appetite of the two friends, and to give them a feeling of strength which they had not experienced for many a day.

Under the influence of this feeling, Jarwin remarked to Cuffy, that "a man could eat a-most anything when hard put to it," and that "it wos now high time to think about goin' ashore."

To which Cuffy replied with a bark, which one might imagine should come from a dog in the last stage of whooping-cough, and with a wag of his tail—not merely at the root thereof, but a distinct wag—that extended obviously along its entire length to the extreme point. Jarwin observed the successful effort, laughed feebly, and said, "Brayvo, Cuffy," with evident delight; for it reminded him of the days when that little shred of a door-mat, in the might of its vigour, was wont to wag its tail so violently as to convulse its whole body, insomuch that it was difficult to decide whether the tail wagged the body, or the body the tail!

But, although Jarwin made light of his sufferings, his gaunt, wasted frame would have been a sad sight to any pitiful spectator, as with weary aspect and unsteady gait he moved about on the sandy ridge in search of more food, or gazed with longing eyes on the richly-wooded island.

For it must be remembered that our castaway had not landed on the island itself, but on that narrow ring of coral-reef which almost encircled it, and from which it was separated by the lagoon, or enclosed portion of the sea, which was, as we have said, about a quarter of a mile wide.

John Jarwin would have thought little of swimming over that narrow belt of smooth water in ordinary circumstances, but now he felt that his strength was not equal to such a feat. Moreover, he knew that there were sharks in these waters, so he dismissed the idea of swimming, and cast about in his mind how he should manage to get across. With Jarwin, action soon followed thought. He resolved to form a small raft out of portions of the large one. Fortunately his clasp-knife had been attached, as seamen frequently have it, to his waist-belt, when he forsook his ship. This was the only implement that he possessed, but it was invaluable. With it he managed to cut the thick ropes that he could not have untied, and, in the course of two hours—for he laboured with extreme difficulty—a few broken planks and spars were lashed together. Embarking on this frail vessel with his dog, he pushed off, and using a piece of plank for an oar, sculled himself over the lagoon.

It was touching, even to himself, to observe the slowness of his progress. All the strength that remained in him was barely sufficient to move the raft. But the lagoon was as still as a millpond. Looking down into its clear depths, he could see the rich gardens of coral and sea-weed, among which fish, of varied and brilliant colours, sported many fathoms below. The air, too, was perfectly calm.

Very slowly he left the reef astern; the middle of the lagoon was gained; then, gradually, he neared the island-shore, but oh! it was a long, weary pull, although the space was so short, and, to add to the poor man's misery, the fish which he had eaten caused him intolerable thirst. But he reached the shore at last.

The first thing that greeted his eye as he landed was the sparkle of a clear spring at the foot of some cocoanut-trees. He staggered eagerly towards it, and fell down beside a hollow in the rock, like a large cup or bowl, which had been scooped out by it.

Who shall presume to describe the feelings of that shipwrecked sailor as he and his dog drank from the same cup at that sparkling crystal fountain? Delicious odours of lime and citron trees, and well-nigh forgotten herbage, filled his nostrils, and the twitter of birds thrilled his ears, seeming to bid him welcome to the land, as he sank down on the soft grass, and raised his eyes in thanksgiving to heaven. An irresistible tendency to sleep then seized him.

"If there's a heaven upon earth, I'm in it now," he murmured, as he laid down his head and closed his eyes.

Cuffy, nestling into his breast, placed his chin on his neck, and heaved a deep, contented sigh. This was the last sound the sailor recognised, as he sank into profound repose.

Chapter Two

Island Life

There are few of the minor sweets of life more agreeable than to awake refreshed, and to become gradually impressed with the conviction that you are a perfectly free agent,—that you may rise when you choose, or lie still if you please, or do what you like, without let or hindrance.

So thought our hero, John Jarwin, when he awoke, on the same spot where he had thrown himself down, after several hours of life-giving slumber. He was still weak, but his weakness did not now oppress him. The slight meal, the long draught, and the deep sleep, had restored enough of vigour to his naturally robust frame to enable him, while lying on his back, to enjoy his existence once more. He was, on first awaking, in that happy condition of mind and body in which the former does not care to think and the latter does not wish to move—yet both are pleased to be largely conscious of their own identity.

That he had not moved an inch since he lay down, became somewhat apparent to Jarwin from the fact that Cuffy's chin still rested immovable on his neck, but his mind was too indolent to pursue the thought. He had not the most remote idea as to where he was, but he cared nothing for that. He was in absolute ignorance of the time of day, but he cared, if possible, still less for that. Food, he knew, was necessary to his existence, but the thought gave him no anxiety. In short, John and his dog were in a state of quiescent felicity, and would probably have remained so for some hours to come, had not the setting sun shone forth at that moment with a farewell gleam so intense, that it appeared to set the world of clouds overhead on fire, converting them into hills and dales, and towering domes and walls and battlements of molten glass and gold. Even to the wearied seaman's sleepy vision the splendour of the scene became so fascinating, that he shook off his lethargy, and raised himself on one elbow.

"Why, Cuffy!" he exclaimed, to the yawning dog, "seems to me that the heavens is a-fire! Hope it won't come on dirty weather before you an' I get up somethin' in the shape o' a hut. That minds me, doggie," he added, glancing slowly round him, "that we must look after prokoorin' of our supper. I do believe we've bin an' slep away a whole day! Well, well, it don't much matter, seein' that we hain't got no dooty for to do—no trick at the wheel, no greasin' the masts—wust of all, no splicin' the main brace, and no grub."

This latter remark appeared to reach the understanding of the dog, for it uttered a melancholy howl as it gazed into its master's eyes.

"Ah, Cuffy!" continued the sailor with a sigh, "you've good reason to yowl, for the half of a rotten fish ain't enough for a dog o' your appetite. Come, let's see if we can't find somethin' more to our tastes."

Saying this the man rose, stretched himself, yawned, looked helplessly round for a few seconds, and then, with a cheery "Hallo! Cuff, come along, my hearty," went down to the beach in quest of food.

In this search he was not unsuccessful, for the beach abounded with shell-fish of various kinds; but Jarwin ate sparingly of these, having been impressed, in former years, by some stories which he had heard of shipwrecked sailors having been poisoned by shell-fish. For the same reason he administered a moderate supply to Cuffy, telling him that "it warn't safe wittles, an' that if they was to be pisoned, it was as well to be pisoned in moderation." The dog, however, did not appear to agree with its master on this point, for it went picking up little tit-bits here and there, and selfishly ignoring the "share-and-share-alike" compact, until it became stuffed alarmingly, and could scarcely follow its master back to the fountain.

Arrived there, the two slaked their thirst together, and then Jarwin sat down to enjoy a pipe, and Cuffy lay down to suffer the well-merited reward of gluttony.

We have said that Jarwin sat down to enjoy a pipe, but he did *not* enjoy it that night, for he discovered that the much-loved little implement, which he had cherished tenderly while on the raft, was broken to atoms in his coat-pocket! In his eagerness to drink on first landing, he had thrown himself down on it, and now smoking was an impossibility, at least for that night. He reflected, however, that it would not be difficult to make a wooden pipe, and that cigarettes might perhaps be made by means of leaves, or bark, while his tobacco lasted; so he consoled himself in the meantime with hopeful anticipations, and a quid. Being still weak and weary, he lay down again beside the fountain, and almost immediately fell into a sleep, which was not at all disturbed by the starts and groans and frequent yelps of Cuffy, whose sufferings could scarcely have been more severe if he had supped on turtle-soup and venison, washed down with port and claret.

Thus did those castaways spend the first night on their island.

It must not be supposed, however, that we are going to trace thus minutely every step and sensation in the career of our unfortunate friends. We have too much to tell that is important to devote our "valuable space" to everyday incidents. Nevertheless, as it is important that our readers should understand our hero thoroughly, and the circumstances in which we find him, it is necessary that we should draw attention to some incidents—trifling in themselves, but important in their effects—which occurred to John Jarwin soon after his landing on the island.

The first of these incidents was, that John one day slipped his foot on a tangle-covered rock, and fell into the sea. A small matter this, you will say, to a man who could swim, and in a climate so warm that a dip, with or without clothes, was a positive luxury. Most true; and had the wetting been all, Jarwin would have had nothing to annoy him; for at the time the accident occurred he had been a week on the island, had managed to pull and crack many cocoa-nuts, and had found various excellent wild-fruits, so that his strength, as well as Cuffy's, had been much restored. In fact, when Jarwin's head emerged from the brine, after his tumble, he gave vent to a shout of laughter, and continued to indulge in hilarious demonstrations all the time he was wringing the water out of his garments, while the terrier barked wildly round him.

But suddenly, in the very midst of a laugh, he became grave and pale,—so pale, that a more obtuse creature than Cuffy might have deemed him ill. While his mouth and eyes slowly opened wider and wider, his hands slapped his pockets, first his trousers, then his vest, then his coat, after which they fell like pistol-shots on his thighs, and he exclaimed, in a voice of horror—"Gone!"

Ay, there could be no doubt about it; every particle of his tobacco was gone! It had never been much, only three or four plugs; but it was strong, and he had calculated that, what with careful husbanding, and mixing it with other herbs, it would last him for a considerable length of time.

In a state bordering on frenzy, the sailor rushed back to the rock from which he had fallen. The "baccy" was not there. He glanced right and left—no sign of it floating on the sea. In he went, head foremost, like a determined suicide; down, down to the bottom, for he was an expert diver, and rioted among the coral groves, and horrified the fish, until he well-nigh burst, and rose to the surface with a groan and splutter that might have roused envy in a porpoise. Then down he went again, while Cuffy stood on the shore regarding him with mute amazement.

Never did pearl-diver grope for the treasures of the deep with more eager intensity than did John Jarwin search for that lost tobacco. He remained under water until he became purple in the face, and, coming to the surface after each dive, stayed only long enough to recharge his lungs with air. How deeply he regretted at that time the fact that man's life depended on so frequent and regular a supply of atmospheric air! How enviously he glanced at the fish which, with open eyes and mouths, appeared to regard him with inexpressible astonishment—as well they might! At last Jarwin's powers of endurance began to give way, and he was compelled to return to the shore, to the great relief of Cuffy, which miserable dog, if it had possessed the smallest amount of reasoning power, must have deemed its master hopelessly insane.

"But why so much ado about a piece of tobacco?" we hear some lady-reader or non-smoker exclaim.

Just because our hero was, and had been since his childhood, an inveterate smoker. Of course we cannot prove our opinion to be correct, but we are inclined to believe that if all the smoke that had issued from Jarwin's lips, from the period of his commencing down to that terrible day when he lost his last plug, could have been collected in one vast cloud, it would have been sufficient to have kept a factory chimney going for a month or six weeks. The poor man knew his weakness. He had several times tried to get rid of the habit which had enslaved him, and, by failing, had come to know the tyrannical power of his master. He had once been compelled by circumstances to forego his favourite indulgence for three entire days, and retained so vivid a recollection of his sufferings that he made up his mind never more to strive for freedom, but to enjoy his pipe as long as he lived—to swim with the current, in fact, and take it easy. It was of no use that several men, who objected to smoking from principle, and had themselves gone through the struggle and come off victorious, pointed out that if he went on at his present rate, it would cut short his life. Jarwin didn't believe *that*. He *felt* well and hearty, and said that he "was too tough, by a long way, to be floored by baccy; besides, if his life was to be short, he saw no reason why it should not be a pleasant one." It was vain for these disagreeable men of principle to urge that when his health began to give way he would not find life very pleasant, and then "baccy" would fail to relieve him. Stuff and nonsense? Did not Jarwin know that hundreds of thousands of *old* men enjoyed their pipes to the very last. He also knew that a great many men had filled early graves owing to the use of tobacco, but he chose to shut his eyes to this fact—moreover, although a great truth, it was a difficult truth to prove.

It was of still less use that those tiresome men of principle demonstrated that the money spent in tobacco would, if accumulated, form a snug little fortune to retire upon in his old age. John only laughed at this. "Wot did he want with a fortin in his old age," he would say; "he would rather work to the last for his three B's—his bread and beer and baccy—an' die in harness. A man couldn't get on like a man without them three B's, and he wosn't goin' for to deprive hisself of none of 'em, not he; besides, his opponents were bad argifiers," he was wont to say, with a chuckle, "for if, as they said, baccy would be the means of cuttin' his life short, why then, he wouldn't never come to old age to use his fortin, even if he *should* manage to save it off his baccy."

This last argument always brought Jarwin off with flying colours—no wonder, for it was unanswerable; and thus he came to love his beer and baccy so much that he became thoroughly enslaved to both.

His brief residence on the south-sea island had taught him, by painful experience, that he *was* capable of existing without at least two of his three B's—bread and beer. He had suffered somewhat from the change of diet; and now that his third B was thus suddenly, unexpectedly, and hopelessly wrenched from him, he sat himself down on the beach beside Cuffy, and gazed out to sea in absolute despair.

We must guard the reader at this point from supposing that John Jarwin had ever been what is called an intemperate man. He was one of those honest, straightforward tars who do their duty like men, and who, although extremely fond of their pipe and their glass of grog, never lower themselves below the level of the brutes by getting drunk. At the same time, we feel constrained to add that Jarwin acted entirely from impulse and kindly feeling. He had little to do with principle, and did not draw towards those who professed to be thus guided. He was wont to say that they "was troublesome fellers, always shovin' in their oars when they weren't wanted to, an' settin' themselves up for better than everybody else." Had one of those troublesome fellows presented John Jarwin with a pound of tobacco in his forlorn circumstances, at that time he would probably have slapped him on the shoulder, and called him one of the best fellows under the sun!

"Cuffy, my friend," exclaimed Jarwin at last, with an explosive sigh, "all the baccy's gone, so we'll have to smoke sea-weed for the futur'." The terrier said "Bow-wow" to this, cocked its ears, and looked earnest, as if waiting for more.

"Come along," exclaimed the man, overturning his dog as he leaped up, "we'll go home and have summat to eat."

Jarwin had erected a rude hut, composed of boughs and turf, near the fountain where he had first landed. It was the home to which he referred. At first he had devoted himself entirely to the erection of this shelter, and to collecting various roots and fruits and shell-fish for food, intending to delay the examination of the island until his strength should be sufficiently restored to enable him to scale the heights without more than ordinary fatigue. He had been so far recruited as to have fixed for his expedition the day following that on which he sustained his irreparable loss.

Entering his hut he proceeded to kindle a fire by means of a small burning-glass, with which, in happier times, he had been wont to light his pipe. Very soon he had several roots, resembling small potatoes, baking in the hot ashes. With these, a handful of plums, a dozen of oyster-like fish, of which there were plenty on the shore, and a draught of clear cold water, he made a hearty repast, Cuffy coming in for a large share of it, as a matter of course. Then he turned all his pockets inside out, and examined them as carefully as if diamonds lurked in the seams. No, not a speck of tobacco was to be found! He smelt them. The odour was undoubtedly strong—very strong. On the strength of it he shut his eyes, and endeavoured to think that he was smoking; but it was a weak substitute for the pipe, and not at all satisfying. Thereafter he sallied forth and wandered about the sea-shore in a miserable condition, and went to bed that night—as he remarked to his dog—in the blues.

Reader, it is not possible to give you an adequate conception of the sensations and sufferings of John Jarwin on that first night of his bereaved condition. He dreamed continuously of tobacco. Now he was pacing the deck of his old ship with a splendid pipe of cut Cavendish between his lips. Anon he was smoking a meerschaum the size of a hogshead, with a stem equal to the length and thickness of the main-topmast of a seventy-four; but somehow the meerschaum wouldn't draw, whereupon John, in a passion, pronounced it worthy of its name, and hove it overboard, when it was instantly transformed into a shark with a cutty pipe in its mouth. To console himself our hero endeavoured to thrust into his mouth a quid of negro-head, which, however, suddenly grew as big as the cabin-skylight, and became as tough as gutta-percha, so that it was utterly impossible to bite off a piece; and, stranger still, when the poor sailor had by struggling got it in, it dwindled down into a point so small that he could not feel it in his mouth at all. On reaching this, the vanishing-point, Jarwin awoke to a consciousness of the dread reality of his destitute condition. Turning on his other side with a deep groan, he fell asleep again, to dream of tobacco in some new and tantalising form until sunrise, when he awoke unrefreshed. Leaping up, he cast off his clothes, rushed down the beach, and plunged into sea, by way of relieving his feelings.

During the day John Jarwin brooded much over his dreams, for his mind was of a reflective turn, and Cuffy looked often inquiringly into his face. That sympathetic doggie would evidently have besought him to pour his sorrows into his cocked ears if he could have spoken; but—alas! for people who are cast away on desert islands—the gift of speech has been denied to dogs.

Besides being moody, Jarwin was uncommonly taciturn that day. He did not tell Cuffy the result of his cogitations, so that we cannot say anything further about them. All that we are certainly sure of is, that he was profoundly miserable that day—that he postponed his intended expedition to the top of the neighbouring hill—that he walked about the beach slowly, with his chin on his breast and his hands in his pockets—that he made various unsuccessful attempts to smoke dried leaves, and bark, and wild-flowers, mixing with those substances shreds of his trousers' pockets, in order that they might have at least the flavour of tobacco—that he became more and more restive as the day wore on, became more submissive in the evening, paid a few apologetic attentions to Cuffy at supper-time, and, finally, went to bed in a better frame of mind, though still craving painfully for the weed which had enslaved him. That night his dreams were still of tobacco! No lover was ever assailed more violently with dreams of his absent mistress than was John Jarwin with longings for his adorable pipe. But there was no hope for him—the beloved one was effectually and permanently gone; so, like a sensible man, he awoke next morning with a stern resolve to submit to his fate with a good grace.

In pursuance of this resolution he began the day with a cold bath, in which Cuffy joined him. Then he breakfasted on chestnuts, plums, citrons, oysters, and shrimps, the former of which abounded in the woods, the latter on the shore. Jarwin caught the shrimps in a net, extemporised out of his pocket-handkerchief. While engaged with his morning meal, he was earnestly watched by several green paroquets with blue heads and crimson breasts; and during pauses in the meal he observed flocks of brightly-coloured doves and wood-pigeons, besides many other kinds of birds, the names of which he did not know, as well as water-hens, plover, and wild ducks.

"Lost your appetite this morning, Cuff?" said Jarwin, offering his companion a citron, which he decidedly refused. "Ah!" he continued, patting the dog's sides, "I see how it is; you've had breakfast already this morning; bin at it when I was a-sleepin'. For shame, Cuffy!—you should have waited for me; an' you've bin an' over-ate yourself again, you greedy dog!"

This was evidently the case. The guilty creature, forgetful of its past experiences, had again gorged itself with dead fish, which it had found on the beach, and looked miserable.

"Well, never mind, doggie," said Jarwin, finishing his meal, and rising. "I'll give you a little exercise to-day for the good of your health. We shan't go sulking as we did yesterday; so, come along."

The sailor left his bower as he spoke, and set off at a round pace with his hands in his pockets, and a thick stick under his arm, whistling as he went, while Cuffy followed lovingly at his heels.

Chapter Three

Communings of Man and Beast

It would appear to be almost an essential element in life that man should indulge in speech. Of course we cannot prove this, seeing that we have never been cast alone on a desert island (although we *have* been next thing to it), and cannot positively conclude what would have been the consequences to our castaway if he had rigidly refrained from speech. All that we can ground an opinion on is the fact that John Jarwin talked as much and as earnestly to his dog as if he knew that that sagacious creature understood every word he uttered. Indeed, he got into such a habit of doing this, that it is very probable he might have come to believe that Cuffy really did understand, though he was not gifted with the power to reply. If it be true that Jarwin came to this state of credulity, certain it is that Cuffy was deeply to blame in the matter, because the way in which that ridiculous hypocrite sat before his master, and looked up in his face with his lustrous, intelligent eyes, and cocked his ears, and wagged his tail, and smiled, might have deceived a much less superstitious man than a British tar.

We have said that Cuffy smiled, advisedly. Some people might object to the word, and say that he only "snickered," or made faces. That, we hold, is a controvertible question. Cuffy's facial contortions looked like smiling. They came very often inappropriately, and during parts of Jarwin's discourse when no smile should have been called forth; but if that be sufficient to prove that Cuffy was not smiling, then, on the same ground, we hold that a large proportion of those ebullitions which convulse the human countenance are not smiles but unmeaning grins. Be this as it may, Cuffy smiled, snickered, or grinned amazingly, during the long discourses that were delivered to him by his master, and indeed looked so wonderfully human in his knowingness, that it only required a speaking tongue and a shaved face to constitute him an unanswerable proof of the truth of the Darwinian theory of the origin of the human species.

"Cuffy," said Jarwin, panting, as he reached the summit of his island, and sat down on its pinnacle rock, "that's a splendid view, ain't it?"

To any one save a cynic or a misanthrope, Cuffy replied with eye and tail, "It is magnificent."

"But you're not looking at it," objected Jarwin, "you're looking straight up in my face; so how can you tell what it's like, doggie?"

"I see it all," replied Cuffy with a grin; "all reflected in the depths of your two loving eyes."

Of course Jarwin lost this pretty speech in consequence of its being a mute reply, but he appeared to have some intuitive perception of it, for he stooped down and patted the dog's head affectionately.

After this there was a prolonged silence, during which the sailor gazed wistfully round the horizon. The scene was indeed one of surpassing beauty and grandeur. The island on which he had been cast was one of those small coral gems which deck the breast of the Pacific. It could not have been more than nine or ten miles in circumference, yet within this area there lay a miniature world. The mountain-top on which the seaman sat was probably eight or nine hundred feet above the level of the sea, and commanded a view of the whole island. On one side lay three lesser hills, covered to their summits with indescribably rich verdure, amongst which rose conspicuous the tall stems and graceful foliage of many cocoanut-palms. Fruit-trees of various kinds glistened in the sunshine, and flowering shrubs in abundance lent additional splendour to the scene. On the other side of the mountain a small lake glittered like a jewel among the trees; and there numerous flocks of wild-fowl disported themselves in peaceful security. From the farther extremity of the lake flowed a rivulet, which, from the mountain-top, resembled a silver thread winding its way through miniature valleys, until lost in the light yellow sand of the sea-shore. On this beach there was not even a ripple, because of the deep calm which prevailed but on the ring or coral-reef, which completely encircled the island, those great "rollers"—which appear never to go down even in calm—fell from time to time with a long, solemn roar, and left an outer ring of milk-white foam. The blue lagoon between the reef and the island varied from a few yards to a quarter of a mile in breadth, and its quiet waters were like a sheet of glass, save where they were ruffled now and then by the diving of a sea-gull or the fin of a shark. Birds of many kinds filled the grove with sweet sounds, and tended largely to dispel that feeling of intense loneliness which had been creeping that day over our seaman's spirit.

"Come, my doggie," said Jarwin, patting his dumb companion's head, "if you and I are to dwell here for long, we've got a most splendid estate to look after. I only hope we won't find South Sea niggers in possession before us, for they're not hospitable, Cuffy, they ain't hospitable, bein' given, so I'm told, to prefer human flesh to most other kinds o' wittles."

He looked anxiously round in all directions at this point, as if the ideas suggested by his words were not particularly agreeable.

"No," he resumed, after a short survey, "it don't seem as if there was any of 'em here. Anyhow I can't see none, and most parts of the island are visible from this here mast-head."

Again the seaman became silent as he repeated his survey of the island; his hands, meanwhile, searching slowly, as if by instinct, round his pockets, and into their most minute recesses, if haply they might find an atom of tobacco. Both hands and eyes, however, failed in their search; so, turning once more towards his dog, Jarwin sat down and addressed it thus:—

"Cuff, my doggie, don't wink in that idiotical way, you hanimated bundle of oakum! and don't wag yer tail so hard, else you'll shake it off some fine day! Well, Cuff, here you an' I are fixed—'it may be for years, an' it may be for ever'—as the old song says; so it behoves you and me to hold a consultation as to wot's the best to be done for to make the most of our sukumstances. Ah, doggie!" he continued in a low tone, looking pensively towards the horizon, "it's little that my dear wife (your missus and mine, Cuff) knows that her John has fallen heir to sitch an estate; become, so to speak, 'monarch of all he surveys.' O Molly, Molly, if you was only here, wot a paradise it would be! Eden over again; Adam an' Eve, without a'most no difference, barrin' the clo'se, by the way, for if I ain't mistaken, Adam didn't wear a straw hat and a blue jacket, with pumps and canvas ducks. Leastwise, I've never heard that he did; an' I'm quite sure that Eve didn't go to church on Sundays in a gown wi' sleeves like two legs o' mutton, an' a bonnet like a coal-scuttle. By the way, I don't think they owned a doggie neither."

At this point the terrier, who had gradually quieted down during the above soliloquy, gave a responsive wag of its tail, and looked up with a smile—a plain, obvious, unquestionable smile, which its master believed in most thoroughly.

"Ah, you needn't grin like that, Cuff," replied Jarwin, "it's quite certain that Adam and Eve had no doggie. No doubt they had plenty of wild 'uns—them as they giv'd names to—but they hadn't a good little tame 'un like you, Cuff; no, nor nobody else, for you're the best dog in the world—if you'd only keep yer spanker-boom quiet; but you'll shake it off, you will, if you go on like that. There, lie down, an' let's get on with our consultation. Well, as I was sayin' when you interrupted me, wot a happy life we could live here if we'd only got the old girl with us! I'd be king, you know, Cuff, and she'd be queen, and we'd make you prime minister—you're prime favourite already, you know. There now, if you don't clap a stopper on that ere spanker-boom, I'll have to lash it down. Well, to proceed: we'd build a hut—or a palace—of turf an' sticks, with a bunk alongside for you; an' w'en our clo'se began for to wear out, we'd make pants and jackets and petticoats of cocoanut-fibre; for you must know I've often see'd mats made o' that stuff, an' splendid wear there's in it too, though it would be rather rough for the skin at first; but we'd get used to that in coorse o' time. Only fancy Mrs Jarwin in a cocoanut-fibre petticoat with a palm-leaf hat, or somethink o' that sort! An', after all, it wouldn't be half so rediklous as some o' the canvas she's used to spread on Sundays."

Jarwin evidently thought his ideas somewhat ridiculous, for he paused at this point and chuckled, while Cuffy sprang up and barked responsively.

While they were thus engaged, a gleam of white appeared on the horizon.

"Sail ho!" shouted the sailor in the loud, full tones with which he was wont to announce such an appearance from the mast-head in days gone by.

Oh, how earnestly he strained his eyes in the direction of that little speck! It might have been a sail; just as likely it was the wing of a sea-gull or an albatross. Whatever it was, it grew gradually less until it sank out of view on the distant horizon. With it sank poor Jarwin's newly-raised hopes. Still he continued to gaze intently, in the hope that it might reappear; but it did not. With a heavy sigh the sailor rose at length, wakened Cuffy, who had gone to sleep, and descended the mountain.

This look-out on the summit of the island now became the regular place of resort for Jarwin and his dumb, but invaluable companion. And so absorbed did the castaway become, in his contemplation of the horizon, and in his expectation of the heaving in sight of another sail, that he soon came to spend most of his time there. He barely gave himself time to cook and eat his breakfast before setting out for the spot, and frequently he remained there the livelong day, having carried up enough of provision to satisfy his hunger.

At first, while there, he employed himself in the erection of a rude flag-staff, and thus kept himself busy and reasonably cheerful. He cut the pole with some difficulty, his clasp-knife being but a poor substitute for an axe; then he bored a hole at the top to reave the halliards through. These latter he easily made by plaiting together threads of cocoanut-fibre, which were both tough and long. When ready, he set up and fixed the staff, and hoisted thereon several huge leaves of the palm-tree, which, in their natural size and shape, formed excellent flags.

When, however, all this was done, he was reduced to a state of idleness, and his mind began to dwell morbidly on the idea of being left to spend the rest of his days on the island. His converse with Cuffy became so sad that the spirits of that sagacious and sympathetic dog were visibly affected. He did, indeed, continue to lick his master's hand lovingly, and to creep close to his side on all occasions; but he ceased to wag his expressive tail with the violence that used to characterise that appendage in other days, and became less demonstrative in his conduct. All this, coupled with constant exposure in all sorts of weather—although Jarwin was not easily affected by a breeze or a wet jacket—began at last to undermine the health of the stout seaman. He became somewhat gaunt and hollow-cheeked, and his beard and moustache, which of course he could not shave, and which, for a long time, presented the appearance of stubble, added to the lugubriosity of his aspect.

As a climax to his distress, he one day lost his dog! When it went off, or where it went to, he could not tell, but, on rousing up one morning and putting out his hand almost mechanically to give it the accustomed pat of salutation, he found that it was gone.

A thrill of alarm passed through his frame on making this discovery, and, leaping up, he began to shout its name. But no answering bark was heard. Again and again he shouted, but in vain. Without taking time to put on his coat, he ran to the top of the nearest eminence, and again shouted loud and long. Still no answer.

A feeling of desperate anxiety now took possession of the man. The bare idea of being left in utter loneliness drove him almost distracted. For some time he ran hither and thither, calling passionately to his dog, until he became quite exhausted; then he sat down on a rock, and endeavoured to calm his spirit and consider what he should do. Indulging in his tendency to think aloud, he said—

"Come now, John, don't go for to make a downright fool of yerself. Cuffy has only taken a longer walk than usual. He'll be home to breakfast; but you may as well look a bit longer, there's no sayin' wot may have happened. He may have felled over a precepiece or sprain'd his leg. Don't you give way to despair anyhow, John Jarwin, but nail yer colours to the mast, and never say die."

Somewhat calmed by these encouraging exhortations, the sailor rose up and resumed his search in a more methodical way. Going down to the sea, he walked thence up to the edge of the bush, gazing with the utmost intensity at the ground all the way, in the hope of discovering Cuffy's fresh footsteps; but none were to be seen.

"Come," said he, "it's clear that you haven't gone to the s'uth'ard o' yer home; now, we'll have a look to the nor'ard."

Here he was more successful. The prints of Cuffy's small paws were discovered on the wet sand bearing northward along shore. Jarwin followed them up eagerly, but, coming to a place where the sand was hard and dry, and covered with thin grass, he lost them.

Turning back to where they were distinct, he recommenced the search. No red Indian, in pursuit of friend or foe, ever followed up a trail with more intense eagerness than poor Jarwin followed the track of his lost companion. He even began to develop, in quite a surprising way, some of the deep sagacity of the savage; for he came, before that day was over, not only to distinguish the prints of Cuffy's paws on pretty hard sand, where the impressions were very faint, but even on rough ground, where there were no distinct marks at all—only such indications as were afforded by the pressure of a dead leaf into soft ground, or the breaking of a fallen twig!

Nevertheless, despite his care, anxiety, and diligence, Jarwin failed to find his dog. He roamed all that day until his limbs were weary, and shouted till his voice was hoarse, but only echoes answered him. At last he sat down, overcome with fatigue and grief.

It had rained heavily during the latter part of the day and soaked him to the skin, but he heeded it not. Towards evening the weather cleared up little, but the sun descended to the horizon in a mass of black clouds, which were gilded with (a) strange lurid light that presaged a storm; while sea-birds flew overhead and shrieked in wild excitement, as if they were alarmed at the prospect before them. But Jarwin observed and cared for none of these things. He buried his face in his hands, and sat for some time perfectly motionless.

While seated thus, a cold shiver passed through his frame once or twice, and he felt unusually faint.

"Humph!" said he, the second time this occurred, "strange sort o' feelin'. Never felt it before. No doubt it's in consikince o' goin' without wittles all day. Well, well," he added, with a deep long-drawn sigh, "who'd have thought I'd lose 'ee, Cuff, in this fashion. It's foolish, no doubt, to take on like this, but I can't help it somehow. I don't believe I could feel much worse if I had lost my old 'ooman. It's kurious, but I feels awful lonesome without 'ee, my doggie."

He was interrupted by the shivering again, and was about to rise, when a long low wail struck on his ear. He listened intently.

No statue ever sat more motionless on its pedestal than did Jarwin during the next three minutes.

Again the wail rose, faint and low at first, then swelling out into a prolonged loud cry, which, strange to say, seemed to be both distant and near.

John Jarwin was not altogether free from superstition. His heart beat hard under the influence of a mingled feeling of hope and fear; but when he heard the cry the third time, he dismissed his fears, and, leaping up, hurried forward in the direction whence the sound appeared to come. The bushes were thick and difficult to penetrate, but he persevered on hearing a repetition of the wail, and was thus led into a part of the island which he had not formerly visited.

Presently he came to something that appeared not unlike an old track; but, although the sun had not quite set, the place was so shut in by tangled bushes and trees that he could see nothing distinctly. Suddenly he put his right foot on a mass of twigs, which gave way under his weight, and he made a frantic effort to recover himself. Next moment, he fell headlong into a deep hole or pit at the bottom of which he lay stunned for some time. Recovering, he found that no bones were broken, and after considerable difficulty, succeeded in scrambling out of the hole. Just as he did so, the wail was again raised; but it sounded so strange, and so unlike any sound that Cuffy could produce, that he was tempted to give up the search—all the more that his recent fall had so shaken his exhausted frame that he could scarcely walk.

While he stood irresolute, the wail was repeated, and, this time, there was a melancholy sort of "bow-wow" mingled with it, that sent the blood careering through his veins like wildfire. Fatigue and hunger were forgotten. Shouting the name of his dog, he bounded forward, and would infallibly have plunged head-foremost into another pit, at the bottom of which Cuffy lay, had not that wise creature uttered a sudden bark of joy, which checked his master on the very brink.

"Hallo! *Cuff*, is that you, my doggie?"

"Bow, wow, *wow*!" exclaimed Cuffy in tones which there could be no mistaking, although the broken twigs and herbage which covered the mouth of the pit muffled them a good deal, and accounted for the strangeness of the creature's howls when heard at a distance.

"Why, where ever have 'ee got yourself into?" said Jarwin, going down on his knees and groping carefully about the opening of the pit. "I do believe you've bin an' got into a trap o' some sort. The savages must have been here before us, doggie, and made more than one of 'em, for I've just comed out o' one myself. Hallo! *there*, I'm into another!" he exclaimed as the treacherous bank gave way, and he slipped in headlong, with a dire crash, almost smothering Cuffy in his fall.

Fortunately, no damage, beyond a few scratches, resulted either to dog or man, and in a few minutes more both stood upon firm ground.

It would be vain, reader to attempt to give you in detail all that John Jarwin said and did on that great occasion, as he sat there on the ground caressing his dog as if it had been his own child. We leave it to your imagination!

When he had expended the first burst of feeling, he got up, and was about to retrace his steps, when he observed some bones lying near him. On examination, these proved to be the skeleton of a man. At first Jarwin thought it must be that of a native; but he was startled to find among the dust on which the skeleton lay several brass buttons with anchors on them. That he stood beside the remains of a brother seaman, who had probably been cast on that island, as he himself had been, seemed very evident, and the thought filled him with strange depressing emotions. As it was by that time too dark to make further investigations, he left the place, intending to return next day; and, going as cautiously as possible out of the wood, returned to his abode, where he kindled a fire, gave Cuffy some food, and prepared some for himself; but before he had tasted that food another of the shivering fits seized him. A strange feeling of being very ill, and a peculiar wandering of his mind, induced him to throw himself on his couch. The prolonged strain to which body and mind had been subjected had proved too much for him, and before morning he was stricken with a raging fever.

Chapter Four

Hopes and Fears and Stern Resolves Lead to Vigorous Action

For several days the sailor lay tossing in helpless misery in his bower, without food or fire. Indeed he could not have eaten even if food had been offered him, and as to fire, there was heat enough in his veins, poor fellow! to more than counterbalance the want of that.

During part of the time he became delirious, and raved about home and sea-life and old companions in a way that evidently quite alarmed Cuffy, for that sagacious terrier approached his master with caution, with his tail between his legs, and a pitiful, earnest gaze, that was quite touching. This was partly owing to the fact that Jarwin had several times patted him with such painful violence as to astonish and render him doubtful of the affection displayed by such caresses. Jarwin also recurred at these times to his tobacco and beer, and apparently suffered a good deal from dreams about those luxuries. In his ravings he often told Cuffy to fill a pipe for him, and advised him to look sharp about it, and he frequently reproached some of his old comrades for not passing the beer. Fortunately the fountain was close at hand, and he often slaked his burning thirst at it. He also thought frequently of the skeleton in the thicket, and sometimes raved with an expression of horror about being left to die alone on a desert island.

By degrees the fever reached its climax, and then left him almost dead. For a whole day and night he lay so absolutely helpless that it cost him an effort to open his eyes, and he looked so ill that the poor dog began to whine piteously over him, but the day after that a sensation of hunger induced him to make an effort to rouse up. He tried to raise his head—it felt as if made of lead.

"Hallo! Cuffy, somethin' wrong I suspect!"

It was the first time for many days that Jarwin had spoken in his natural tones. The effect on the dog was instantaneous and powerful. It sprang up, and wagged its expressive tail with something of the energy of former times; licked the sick man's face and hands; whined and barked intelligently; ran away in little bursts, as if it had resolved to undertake a journey off-hand, but came back in a few seconds, and in many other ways indicated its intense delight at finding that Jarwin was "himself again."

But alas! Jarwin was not quite himself yet, and Cuffy, after his first ebullition, sat looking in surprise at the invalid, as he strove to turn on his side, and reach out his heavy hand and skinny arm towards a few scraps of the last meal he had cooked before being struck down. Cuffy, after eating the portion of that meal that suited his taste, had left the remnants there as being unworthy of notice, and catered for himself among the dead fish cast up on the beach. Although lying within a yard of his couch, Jarwin had the greatest difficulty in reaching the food; and when he did at length succeed in grasping it, he fell back on his couch, and lay for a long time as if dead. Soon, however, he recovered, and, with a feeling of gratitude such as he had never before experienced, began to gnaw the hard morsels.

"I'm in a bad way, Cuff," he said, after satisfying the first cravings of hunger.

Cuffy gave a responsive wag with his tail, and cocked his ears for more.

"Hows'ever, seems to me that I've got the turn; let's be thankful for *that*, my doggie. Wonder how long I've bin ill. Months mayhap. Don't think I could have come to be sitch a skeleton in a short time. Ha! that minds me o' the skeleton in the wood. Have 'ee seed it, Cuff, since I found 'ee there? Well, I must eat and drink too, if I would keep the skin on *my* skeleton. Wish you had hands, doggie, for I'm greatly in need o' help just now. But you're a comfort, anyhow, even though you hain't got no hands. I should have died without you, my doggie—you cheer me up, d'ee see, and when it's nigh low water with a man, it don't take much to make him slip his cable. The want of a kind look at this here time, Cuffy, would have sent me adrift, I do believe."

It must not be supposed that all this was spoken fluently. It came slowly, by fits and starts, with a long pause at the end of each sentence, and with many a sigh between, expressive of extreme weakness.

"I wish I had a drink, Cuffy," said the invalid after a long pause, turning a longing look towards the spring, which welled up pleasantly close to the opening of the hut. "Ay, that's all very well in its way, but bow-wowin' an' waggin' yer tail won't fetch me a can o' water. Hows'ever, it's o' no manner o' use wishin'. 'Never say die.' Here goes."

So saying, he began slowly and painfully, but with unyielding perseverance, to push, and draw, and hitch himself, while lying at full length, towards the spring, which he reached at last so exhausted, that he had barely put his lips to it and swallowed a mouthful, when his head dropped, and he almost fainted. He was within an ace of being drowned, but with a violent effort he drew his face out of the spring, and lay there in a half unconscious condition for some time, with the clear cool water playing about his temples. Reviving in a little time, he took another sip, and then crawled back to his couch. Immediately he fell into a profound slumber, from which Cuffy strove in vain to awaken him; therefore, like a sagacious dog, he lay down at his master's side and joined him in repose.

From that hour Jarwin began to mend rapidly. In a few days he was able to walk about with the aid of a stick. In a few weeks he felt somewhat like his former self, and soon after that, he was able to ascend to the top of the island, and resume his watch for a passing sail. But the first few hours of his watch beside the old flagstaff convinced him that his hopes would, in all probability, be doomed to disappointment, and that he would soon fall back into a state of apathy, from which he might perhaps be unable to rouse himself, in which case his fate would certainly be that of the poor sailor whose remains he had that day buried in the pit near to which they had been discovered. He resolved, therefore, to give up watching altogether, and to devote all his energies in future to devising some plan of escape from the island, but when he bent his mind to this task he felt a deep sinking of the heart, for he had no implements wherewith to construct a boat or canoe.

Suddenly it occurred to him, for the first time in his life, that he ought, in this extremity, to pray to God for help. He was, as we have said, a straightforward man, prompt to act as well as ready to conceive. He fell on his knees at once, humbly confessed his sin in depending so entirely on himself in time past, and earnestly asked help and guidance for the future. His prayer was not long—neither was the publican's—but it was effectual. He arose with feelings of strong resolution and confidence, which appeared to himself quite unaccountable, for he had not, as yet, conceived any new idea or method as to escaping from the island. Instead of setting his mind to work, as he had intended, he could not help dwelling on the fact that he had never before deliberately asked help from his Maker, and this raised a train of self-condemnatory thoughts which occupied him the remainder of that day. At night he prayed again before laying down to rest.

Next morning he rose like a giant refreshed, and, after a plunge in the sea and a hearty breakfast, set out with Cuffy for a meditative walk.

Great were the thoughts that swelled the seaman's broad chest during that walk, and numerous, as well as wild and quaint, were the plans of escape which he conceived and found it necessary to abandon.

"It's harder work to think it out than I had expected, Cuffy," he said, sitting down on a cliff that overlooked the sea, and thinking aloud. "If you and I could only swim twenty miles or so at a stretch, I'd risk it; but, as nothin' short o' that would be likely to be of sarvice, we must give it up. Then, if I could only cut down trees with my shoe, and saw planks with my jacket, we might make a boat; but I can't do that, and we haven't no nails—except our toe-nails, which ain't the right shape or strong enough; so we must give that up too. It's true that we might burn a canoe out of a solid tree, but who's to cut down the solid tree for us, doggie? I'm sure if the waggin' of a tail could do it you wouldn't be long about it! Why on earth can't 'ee keep it still for a bit? Well, then, as we can't swim or fly, and haven't a boat or canoe, or the means o' makin' em, what's the next thing to be done?"

Apparently neither man nor dog could return an answer to that question, for they both sat for a very long time in profound silence, staring at the sea.

After some time Jarwin suddenly exclaimed, "I'll do it!"

Cuffy, startled by the energy with which it was said, jumped up and said, "That's right!"—or something very like it—with his eyes.

"Yes, Cuffy, I'll make a raft, and you and I shall get on it, some day, with a fair wind, and make for the island that we think we've seen so often on the horizon."

He alluded here to a faint blue line which, on unusually fine and clear days, he had distinguished on the horizon to the southward, and which, from its always appearing on the same spot, he believed to be land of some sort, although it looked nothing more than a low-lying cloud.

"So that's settled," continued Jarwin, getting up and walking smartly back to his hut with the air of a man who has a purpose in view. "We shall make use of the old raft, as far as it'll go. Luckily the sail is left, as you and I know, Cuff, for it has been our blanket for many a day, and when all's ready we shall go huntin', you and I, till we've got together a stock of provisions, and then—up anchor and away! We can only be drownded once, you know, and it's better that than stopping here to die o' the blues. What think 'ee o' that, my doggie?"

Whatever the doggie thought of the idea, there can be no question what he thought of the cheery vigorous tones of his master's voice, for he gambolled wildly round, barked with vociferous delight, and wagged his "spanker boom" to such an extent that Jarwin warned him to have a care lest it should be carried away, an' go slap overboard.

In pursuance of the designs thus expressed, the sailor began the construction of a raft without delay, and worked at it diligently the remainder of that day. He found, on examination, that a considerable portion of the old raft yet remained stranded on the beach, though all the smaller spars of which it had been composed had been used for firewood. With great difficulty he rolled these logs one by one into the sea, and, getting astride of each, pushed them by means of a pole towards a point of rocks, or natural jetty, alongside of which the water was deep. Here he fastened them together by means of a piece of rope—one of the old fastenings which remained to him, the others having been used in the construction of the hut. The raft thus formed was, however, much too small to weather a gale or float in a rough sea. In whatever way he placed the spars the structure was too narrow for safety. Seeing, therefore, that it was absolutely necessary to obtain more logs, he set brain and hands to work without delay.

Many years before, he had seen an ancient stone hatchet in a museum, the head of which was fastened to the haft by means of a powerful thong of untanned hide. He resolved to make a hatchet of this sort. Long did he search the beach for a suitable stone, but in vain. At last he found one pretty nearly the proper shape, which he chipped and ground into the rude form of an axe. It had no eye for the handle. To have made a hole in it would have weakened the stone too much. He therefore cut a groove in the side of the handle, placed the head of the stone into it, and completed the fastening by tying it firmly with the tough fibrous roots of a tree. It was strongly and neatly made, though clumsy in appearance, but, do what he would, he could not put a sufficiently fine edge on it, and although it chipped pretty well when applied to the outside of a tree, it made very slow progress indeed as the cut deepened, and the work became so toilsome at last that he almost gave it up in despair. Suddenly it occurred to him that fire might be made use of to facilitate the work. Selecting a tall cocoanut-tree, he piled dry wood all round the foot of it. Before setting it on fire he dipped a quantity of cocoanut fibre in the sea and tied a thick belt of this round the tree just above the pile, so as to protect the upper parts of the spar from the flames as much and as long as possible. This done, he kindled the pile. A steady breeze fanned the flame into an intense fire, which ere long dried up the belt of fibre and finally consumed it. The fire was pretty well burnt out by that time, however, so that the upper part of the stem had been effectually preserved. Removing the ashes, he was rejoiced to find that the foot of the tree had been so deeply burned that several inches of it were reduced to charcoal, which his stone hatchet readily cut away, and the operation was so successful that it only required a second fire to enable him to fell the tree.

This done, he measured it off in lengths. Under each point of measurement he piled up dry wood—which consisted merely of broken branches—with belts of wet fibre on each side of these piles. Then, applying a light to the fires he reduced the parts to charcoal as before, and completed the work with the hatchet. Thus, in the course of a single day, he felled a tall tree and cut it up into six lengths, which he rolled down to the sea and floated off to the end of the jetty.

Next day Jarwin rose with the sun, and began to make twine of twisted cocoanut fibre—of which there was great abundance to be had everywhere. When a sufficient quantity had been made he plaited the twine into cords, and the cords into stout ropes, which, although not so neat as regular ropes, were, nevertheless, sufficiently pliable and very strong. Several days were spent over this somewhat tedious process; and we may mention here, that in all these operations the busy seaman was greatly assisted by his dog, who stuck close to him all the time, encouraging him with looks and wags of approbation.

After the ropes were made, the raft was put together and firmly lashed. There was a mast and yard in the centre of it, and also a hollow, formed by the omission of a log, which was just large enough to permit of the man and his dog lying down. This hollow, slight though it was, afterwards proved of the utmost service.

It is needless to recount all the details of the building and provisioning of this raft. Suffice it to say that, about three weeks after the idea of it had been conceived, it was completed and ready for sea.

During his residence on the island, although it had only extended over a few months, Jarwin had become very expert in the use of a sharp-pointed pole, or javelin, with which he had become quite an adept in spearing fish. He had also become such a dead-shot with a stone that when he managed to get within thirty yards of a bird, he was almost certain to hit it. Thus he was enabled to procure fish and fowl as much as he required and as the woods abounded with cocoa-nuts, plums, and other wild fruits, besides many edible roots, he had no lack of good fare. Now that he was about to "go to sea," he bethought him of drying some of the fruits as well as curing some fish and birds. This he did by degrees, while engaged on the raft, so that when all was ready he had a store of provisions sufficient to last him several weeks. In order to stow all this he removed another log from the middle of the raft, and, having deposited the food in the hollow—carefully wrapped in cocoanut leaves and made into compact bundles—he covered it over by laying a layer of large leaves above it and lashing a small spar on the top of them to keep them down. The cask with which he had landed from the original raft, and which he had preserved with great care, not knowing how soon he might be in circumstances to require it, served to hold fresh water.

On a fine morning about sunrise, Jarwin embarked with his little dog and bade farewell to the coral island, and although he had not dwelt very long there, he felt, to his own surprise, much regret at quitting it.

A fresh breeze was blowing in the direction of the island—or the supposed island—he wished to reach. This was important, because, in such a craft, it was impossible to sail in any way except before the wind. Still, by means of a rude oar or paddle, he could modify its direction so as to steer clear of the passage through the reef and get out to sea.

Once outside, he squared the sail and ran right before the breeze. Of course such a weighty craft went very slowly through the water, but the wind was pretty strong, and to Jarwin, who had been for a comparatively long time unaccustomed to moving on the water, the speed seemed fast enough. As the island went astern, and the raft lifted and fell gently on the long swell of the ocean, the seaman's heart beat with a peculiar joy to which it had long been a stranger, and he thanked God fervently for having so soon answered his prayer.

For a long time he sat reclining in the hollow of the raft, resting his hand lightly on the steering oar and gazing in silence at the gradually fading woods of his late home. The dog, as if it were aware that a great change was being effected in their destiny, lay also perfectly still—and apparently contemplative—at his master's feet; resting his chin on a log and gazing at the receding land. It was evident, however, that *his* thoughts were not absent or wandering, for, on the slightest motion made by his master, his dark eyes turned towards him, his ears slightly rose, and his tail gave the faintest possible indication of an intention to wag.

"Well, Cuffy," said Jarwin at last, rousing himself with a sigh, "wot are 'ee thinking of?"

The dog instantly rose, made affectionate demonstrations, and whined.

"Ah, you may well say that, Cuff," replied the man; "I know you ain't easy in yer mind, and there's some reason in that, too, for we're off on a raither uncertain viage, in a somewhat unseaworthy craft. Howsever, cheer up, doggie. Whoever turns up, you and I shall sink or swim together."

Just then the sail flapped.

"Hallo! Cuff," exclaimed Jarwin, with a look of anxiety, "the wind's going to shift."

This was true. The wind did shift, and in a few minutes had veered so much round that the raft was carried away from the blue line on the horizon, which Jarwin had so fondly hoped would turn out to be an inhabited island. It blew lightly, however, and when the sun went down, had completely died away. In these circumstances Jarwin and his dog supped together, and then lay down to rest, full of sanguine hope.

They were awakened during the night by a violent squall, which, however, did no further damage than wash a little spray over them, for Jarwin had taken the precaution to lower and make fast the sail. He now turned his attention to preparing the raft for rough weather. This consisted in simply drawing over the hollow— in which he, his dog, and his provisions lay—a piece of canvas that he had cut off the sail, which was unnecessarily large. It served as a tarpaulin, and effectually shielded them from ordinary sprays, but when the breeze freshened to a gale, and green seas swept over the *raft*, it leaked so badly, that Jarwin's cabin became a salt-water bath, and his provisions by degrees were soaked.

At first he did not mind this much, for the air and water were sufficiently warm, but after being wet for several hours he began feel chilled. As for poor Cuffy, his trembling body bore testimony to the state of his feelings; nevertheless he did not complain, being a dog of high spirit and endurance. In these circumstances the seaman hailed the rising sun with great joy, even although it rose in the midst of lurid murky clouds, and very soon hid its face altogether behind them, as if it had made up its mind that the state of things below was so bad as to be not worth shining upon.

All that day and night the gale continued, and they were driven before it. The waves rushed so continuously and furiously over the raft, that it was with the utmost difficulty Jarwin could retain his position on it. Indeed it would have been impossible for him to have done so, if he had not taken the precaution of making the hollow in the centre, into which he could crouch, and thus avoid the full force of the seas. Next day the wind abated a little, but the sea still rolled "mountains high." In order to break their force a little, he ventured to show a little corner of the sail. Small though it was, it almost carried away the slender mast, and drove the raft along at a wonderfully rapid rate.

At last the gale went down, and, finally, it became a dead calm, leaving the raft like a cork heaving on the mighty swell of the Pacific Ocean. Weary and worn—almost dead with watching and exposure—John Jarwin lay down and slept, but his slumber was uneasy and unrefreshing. Sunrise awoke him, and he sat up with a feeling of deep thankfulness, as he basked once more in its warm rays and observed that the sky above him was bright blue. But other feelings mingled with these when he gazed round on the wide waste of water, which still heaved its swelling though now unruffled breast, as if panting after its recent burst of fury.

"Ho! Cuffy—what's that? Not a sail, eh?" exclaimed Jarwin, suddenly starting up, while his languid eyes kindled with excitement.

He was right. After a long, earnest, anxious gaze, he came to the conclusion that it *was* a sail which shone, white and conspicuous, like a speck or a snow-flake on the horizon.

Chapter Five

Jarwin and Cuffy Fall into Bad Company

Immediately on discovering the sail, Jarwin hoisted a small canvas flag, which he had prepared for the purpose, to the mast-head, and then sat down to watch with indescribable earnestness the motions of the vessel. There was great cause for anxiety he well knew, because his raft was a mere speck on the great waste of waters which might easily be overlooked even by a vessel passing at a comparatively short distance, and if the vessel's course should happen to lie across that of the raft, there was every probability she would only be visible for a short time and then pass away like a ray of hope dying out.

After gazing in perfect silence for half-an-hour, Jarwin heaved a deep sigh and said—

"She steers this way, Cuffy."

Cuffy acknowledged the remark with a little whine and a very slight wag of his tail. It was evident that his spirits had sunk to a low ebb, and that he was not prepared to derive comfort from every trifling circumstance.

"Come, we'll have a bit of summat to eat, my doggie," said the sailor, reaching forward his hand to the provision bundle.

Thoroughly understanding and appreciating this remark, Cuffy roused himself and looked on with profound interest, while his master cut up a dried fish. Having received a large share of it, he forgot everything else, and devoted all his powers, physical and mental, to the business in hand. Although Jarwin also applied himself to the food with the devotion of a man whose appetite is sharp, and whose strength needs recruiting, he was very far indeed from forgetting other things. He kept his eyes the whole time on the approaching sail, and once or twice became so absorbed and so anxious lest the vessel should change her course, that he remained with his mouth half open, and with the unconsumed morsel reposing therein for a minute or more at a time.

But the vessel did not change her course. On she came; a fine large schooner with raking masts, and so trim and neat in her rig that she resembled a pleasure-yacht. As she drew near, Jarwin rose, and holding on to the mast, waved a piece of canvas, while Cuffy, who felt that there was now really good ground for rejoicing, wagged his tail and barked in an imbecile fashion, as if he didn't exactly know whether to laugh or cry.

"We're all safe now, doggie," exclaimed Jarwin, as the schooner came cutting through the water before a light breeze, leaving a slight track of foam in her wake.

When within about two or three hundred yards of the raft, the castaway could see that a figure leant on the vessel's side and brought a telescope to bear on him. With a feeling of irrepressible gladness he laughed and waved his hand.

"Ay, ay, take a good squint," he shouted, "an' then lower a boat—eh!—"

He stopped abruptly, for at that moment the figure turned towards the steersman; the schooner's head fell away, presenting her stern to the raft, and began to leave her behind.

The truth flashed upon Jarwin like a thunderbolt. It was clear that the commander of the strange vessel had no intention of relieving him. In the first burst of mingled despair and indignation, the seaman uttered a bass roar of defiance that might have done credit to the lungs of a small carronade, and at the same time shook his fist at the retiring schooner.

The effect of this was as sudden as it was unexpected. To his surprise he observed that the schooner's head was immediately thrown up into the wind, and all her sails shook for a few moments, then, filling out again, the vessel bent gracefully over on the other tack. With returning joy the castaway saw her run straight towards him. In a few minutes she was alongside, and her topsails were backed.

"Look out! catch hold!" cried a gruff voice, as a sailor sent a coil of rope whirling over the raft. Jarwin caught it, took a turn round the mast, and held on.

In a minute the raft was alongside. Weak though he was, Jarwin retained enough of his sailor-like activity to enable him to seize a rope and swing himself on board with Cuffy in his arms.

He found himself on the pure white deck of a craft which was so well appointed and so well kept, that his first impressions were revived—namely, that she was a pleasure-yacht. He knew that she was not a vessel of war, because, besides the absence of many little things that mark such a vessel, the few men on deck were not clothed like man-of-war's-men, and there was no sign of guns, with the exception of one little brass carronade, which was probably used as a signal-gun.

A tall stout man, in plain costume, which was neither quite that of a seaman nor a landsman, stood with his arms crossed on his broad chest near the man at the wheel. To him, judging him to be the captain or owner of the vessel, Jarwin went up, and, pulling his forelock by way of salutation, said—

"Why, sir, I thought 'ee was a-goin' to leave me!"

"So I was," answered the captain, drily. "Hold on to the raft," he added, turning to the man who had thrown the rope to Jarwin.

"Well, sir," said the latter in some surprise, "in course I don't know why you wos a-goin' to leave a feller-creetur to his fate, but I'm glad you didn't go for to do it, 'cos it wouldn't have bin Christian-like. But I'm bound for to thank 'ee, sir, all the same for havin' saved me—and Cuffy."

"Don't be too free with your thanks, my good man," returned the captain, "for you're not saved, as you call it, yet."

"Not saved yet?" repeated Jarwin.

"No. Whether I save you or not depends on your keeping a civil tongue in your head, and on your answers to my questions."

The captain interlarded his speech with many oaths, which, of course, we omit. This, coupled with his rude manners, induced

Jarwin to suspect that the vessel was not a pleasure-yacht after all, so he wisely held his peace.

"Where do you belong to?" demanded the captain.

"To Yarmouth, sir."

"What ship did you sail in, what has come of her, and how came you to be cast adrift?"

"I sailed in the *Nancy*, sir, from Plymouth, with a miscellaneous cargo for China. She sprung a leak in a gale, and we was 'bliged to make a raft, the boats bein' all stove in or washed away. It was barely ready when the ship went down starn foremost. Durin' the gale all my mates were washed off the raft or died of exposure; only me and my dog left."

"How long ago was that?" asked the captain.

"Couldn't rightly say, sir, I've lost count o' time, but it's more than a year gone by anyhow."

"That's a lie," said the captain, with an oath.

"No, 'taint, sir," replied Jarwin, reddening, "it's a truth. I was nigh starved on that raft, but was cast on an island where I've bin till a few days ago ever since, when I put to sea on the raft that now lays a-starn there."

For a few seconds the captain made no rejoinder, but a glance at the raft seemed to satisfy him of the truth of what was said. At length he said abruptly—

"What's your name?"

"John Jarwin, sir."

"Well, John Jarwin, I'll save you on one condition, which is, that you become one of my crew, and agree to do my bidding and ask no questions. What say you?"

Jarwin hesitated.

"Haul up the raft and let this man get aboard of it," said the captain, coolly but sternly, to the seaman who held the rope.

"You've no occasion to be so sharp, sir," said John, remonstratively. "If you wos to tell me to cut my own throat, you

- 41 -

know, I could scarce be expected for to do it without puttin' a few questions as to the reason why. You're a trader, I suppose?"

"Yes, I'm a trader," replied the captain, "but I don't choose to be questioned by you. All you've got to do is to agree to my proposal or to walk over the side. To tell you the truth, when I saw you first through the glass, you looked such a starved wretch that I thought you'd be of no use to me, and if it hadn't been for the yell you gave, that showed there was something in you still, I'd have left you to sink or swim. So you see what sort of man you've got to deal with. I'm short-handed, but not so short as to engage an unwilling man, or a man who wouldn't be ready for any sort of dirty work. You may take your choice."

"Well, sir," replied Jarwin, "I've no objection to take service with 'ee. As the sayin' goes, 'beggars mustn't be choosers.' I ain't above doin' dirty work, if required."

John Jarwin, in the simplicity of his heart, imagined that the captain was in need of a man who could and would turn his hand to any sort of work, whether nautical or otherwise, on board ship or ashore, which was his idea of "dirty work;" but the captain appeared to understand him in a different sense, for he smiled in a grim fashion, nodded his head, and, turning to the seaman before mentioned, bade him cut the raft adrift. The man obeyed, and in a few minutes it was out of sight astern.

"Now, Jarwin, go below," said the captain; "Isaacs will introduce you to your messmates."

Isaacs, who had just cut away the raft, was a short, thick-set man, with a dark, expressionless face. He went forward without saying a word, and introduced Jarwin to the men as a "new 'and."

"And a green un, I s'pose; give us your flipper, lad," said one of the crew, holding out his hand.

Jarwin shook it, took off his cap and sat down, while his new friends began, as they expressed it, to pump him. Having no objection to be pumped, he had soon related the whole of his recent history. In the course of the narrative he discovered that his new associates were an unusually rough set. Their language was interspersed with frightful oaths, and their references to the captain showed that his power over them was certainly not founded on goodwill or affection. Jarwin also discovered that the freeness of his communication was not reciprocated by his new mates, for when he made inquiries as to the nature of the trade in which they were engaged, some of the men merely replied with uproarious laughter, chaff, or curses, while others made jocular allusions to sandal-wood trading, slaving, etcetera.

"I shouldn't wonder now," said one, "if you was to think we was pirates."

Jarwin smiled as he replied, "Well, I don't exactly think *that*, but I'm bound for to say the schooner *has* got such a rakish look that it wouldn't seem unnatural like if you *were* to hoist a black flag at the peak. An' you'll excuse me, shipmets, if I say that yer lingo ain't just so polished as it might be."

"And pray who are *you*, that comes here to lecture us about our lingo?" cried one of the men fiercely, starting up and confronting Jarwin with clenched fists.

"Why, mate," replied Jarwin, quietly folding back the cuffs of his coat, and putting himself in an attitude of defence, "I ain't nobody in partikler, not the Lord Chancellor o' England, anyhow still less the Archbishop of Canterbury. I'm only plain Jack Jarwin, seaman, but if you or any other man thinks—"

"Come, come," cried one of the men in a tone of authority, starting forward and thrusting Jarwin's assailant violently aside, "none o' that sort o' thing here. Keep your fists for the niggers, Bill, we're all brothers here, you know; an affectionate family, so to speak!"

There was a general laugh at this. Bill retired sulkily, and Jarwin sat down to a plate of hot "lob-scouse," which proved to be very good, and of which he stood much in need.

For several days our hero was left very much to himself. The schooner sped on her voyage with a fair wind, and the men were employed in light work, or idled about the deck. No one interfered with Jarwin, but at the same time no one became communicative. The captain was a very silent man, and it was evident that the crew stood much in awe of him. Of course Jarwin's suspicions as to the nature of the craft were increased by all this, and from some remarks which he overheard two or three days after his coming on board, he felt convinced that he had fallen into bad company. Before a week had passed, this became so evident that he made up his mind to leave the vessel at the very first opportunity.

One day he went boldly to the captain and demanded to know the nature of the trade in which the schooner was employed and their present destination. He was told that that was no business of his, that he had better go forward and mind his duty without more ado, else he should be pitched overboard. The captain used such forcible language when he said this, and seemed so thoroughly in earnest, that Jarwin felt no longer any doubt as to his true character.

"I'll tell you what it is, my lad," said the captain, "my schooner is a trader or a man-of-war according to circumstances, and I'm a free man, going where I choose and doing what I please. I treat my men well when they do their duty; when they don't I make 'em walk the plank. No doubt you know what that means. If you don't we shall soon teach you. Take to-night to think over it. To-morrow morning I'll have a question or two to ask you. There—go!"

Jarwin bowed submissively and retired.

That night the moon shone full and clear on the wide ocean's breast, and Jarwin stood at the bow of the schooner, looking sadly over the side, and patting his little dog gently on the head.

"Cuffy, you and me's in a fix, I suspect," he murmured in a low tone; "but cheer up, doggie, a way to escape will turn up no doubt."

He had scarcely uttered the words when his eye fell on the distant outline of land on the lee bow. He started, and gazed with fixed intensity for some minutes, under the impression that it might perhaps be a fog-bank lighted by the moon, but in a short time it became so distinct that there could be no doubt it was land. He pointed it out to the watch on deck, one of whom said carelessly that he had seen it for some time, and that there were plenty more islands of the same sort in these seas.

Jarwin walked aft and stood near the lee gangway contemplating the island in silence for some time. A small oar lay at his feet. Suddenly he conceived the daring idea of seizing this, plunging overboard and attempting to swim to land. He was a splendid swimmer, and although the island appeared to be more than two miles distant, he did not fear failure. A moment's reflection, however, convinced him that the men on deck would certainly hear the plunge, heave the ship to, and lower a boat, in which case he should be immediately overtaken. Still, being resolved to escape at all hazards, he determined to make the venture. Fastening a rope to a belaying pin, he tied the oar to it and lowered it over the side until it trailed in the water, he then lifted Cuffy, who was almost always near him, on to the side of the vessel, with a whisper to keep still. The watch paced the weather side of the deck conversing in low tones. The steersman could, from his position, see both gangways, and although the light was not strong enough to reveal what Jarwin was about, it was too strong to admit of his going bodily over the side without being observed. He, therefore, walked slowly to the head of the vessel, where he threw over the end of a small rope. By means of this, when the watch were well aft, he slid noiselessly into the sea, hanging on by one hand and supporting Cuffy with the other. Once fairly in the water he let go, the side of the vessel rubbed swiftly past him, and he all but missed grasping the oar which trailed at the gangway. By this he held on for a few seconds to untie the rope. He had just succeeded and was about to let go, when, unfortunately, the handle of the oar chanced to hit the end of Cuffy's nose a severe blow. The poor dog, therefore, gave vent to a loud yell of pain. Instantly Jarwin allowed himself to sink and held his breath as long as he possibly could, while Cuffy whined and swam on the surface.

Meanwhile the men on deck ran to the side. "Hallo!" cried one, "it's Jarwin's little dog gone overboard."

"Let it go," cried another with a laugh; "it's a useless brute and eats a power o' grub."

"I say, wot a splashin' it do kick up," he added as the little dog was left astern making vain efforts to clamber on the oar. "Why, lads, there's somethin' else floatin' beside it, uncommon like a seal. Are 'ee sure, Bill, that Jarwin hasn't gone overboard along with his dog?"

"Why no," replied Bill; "I seed him go forward a little ago; besides it ain't likely he'd go over without givin' a shout."

"I dun know that," said the other; "he might have hit his head again' somethin' in tumblin' over."

By this time the objects in question were almost out of sight astern. In a few minutes more a dark cloud covered the moon and effectually shut them out from view.

Just then the Captain came on deck, and asked what was wrong.

"Fools!" he exclaimed, in a voice of thunder, on being told, "lower the gig. Look sharp! Don't you see the land, you idiots? The man's away as well as the dog."

In a few seconds the topsails were backed and the boat lowered, manned, and pushed off.

But Jarwin heard and saw nothing of all this. He was now far astern, for the vessel had been going rapidly through the water.

On coming to the surface after his dive he caught hold of Cuffy, and, with a cheering word or two, placed him on his back, telling him to hold on by his paws the best way he could. Then grasping the end of the oar, and pointing the blade land-wards, he struck out vigorously with his legs.

It was a long and weary swim, but as his life depended on it, the seaman persevered. When he felt his strength giving way, he raised not only his heart but his voice in prayer to God, and felt restored each time that he did so. Just as he neared the shore, the sound of oars broke on his ears, and presently he heard the well-known voice of the Captain ordering the men to pull hard. Fortunately it was by this time very dark. He landed without being discerned. The surf was heavy, but he was expert in rough water, went in on the top of a billow, and was safely launched on a soft sandy beach, almost at the same moment with the boat. The latter was, however, at a considerable distance from him. He crept cautiously up the shore until he gained a thicket, and then, rising, he plunged into the woods and ran straight before him until he was exhausted, carrying the little dog in his arms. Many a fall and bruise did the poor fellow receive in his progress, but the fear of being retaken by the pirates—for such he felt convinced they were—lent him wings. The Captain and his men made a long search, but finally gave it up, and, returning to the boat, pushed off. Jarwin never saw them again.

He and Cuffy lay where they had fallen, and slept, wet though they were, till the sun was high. They were still sleeping when a native chief of the island, happening to pass along the beach, discerned Jarwin's footsteps and traced him out. This chief was an immensely large powerful man, armed with a heavy club. He awoke the sailor with a kick, and spoke in a language which he did not understand. His gestures, however, said plainly enough, "Get up and come along with me," so Jarwin thought it best to obey. Of course whatever Jarwin thought, Cuffy was of precisely the same opinion. They therefore quietly got up and followed the big chief to his village, where they were received by a large concourse of savages with much excitement and curiosity.

Chapter Six

Our Hero Becomes a Favourite, and Entertains Hopes of Escape

The sufferings which Jarwin with his little dog had hitherto undergone were as nothing compared to those which he endured for some months after being taken prisoner by the savages. At first he gave himself up for lost, feeling assured that ere long he would be sacrificed in the temple of one of their idols, and then baked in an oven and consumed as food, according to the horrible practice of the South-Sea Islanders. Indeed he began to be much astonished that, as day after day passed, there was no sign of any intention to treat him in this way, although several times the natives took him out of the hut in which he was imprisoned, and, placing him in the centre of a circle, held excited and sometimes angry discussions over him.

It was not till months afterwards, when he had acquired a slight knowledge of their language, that he came to understand why he was spared at this time. It appeared that four shipwrecked sailors, who had been cast on a neighbouring island, had been killed, baked, and eaten, according to usage, by the chief and his friends. Immediately afterwards, those who had partaken of this dreadful food had been seized with severe illness, and one or two had died. This fact had been known for some time to Jarwin's captors, and the discussions above referred to had been engaged in with reference to the question whether it was likely that the flesh of the white man who had been thrown on their island would be likely to disagree with their stomachs! It was agreed that this was highly probable, and thus the seaman's life was spared; but he was sometimes tempted to wish that it had not been spared, for his master, the Big Chief, was a very hard man; he put him to the most toilsome labour, and treated him with every sort of indignity. Moreover, he was compelled to be a witness of practices so revolting and cruel, that he often put the question to himself whether it was possible for devils to display greater wickedness and depravity than these people.

Jarwin was frequently tempted to resent the treatment he received, but, fortunately, he was prudent enough to bear it submissively, for it is certain that if he had rebelled he would have been slain on the spot. Moreover, he set himself to carry out his favourite maxim—namely, that it was wise in all circumstances to make the best of everything. He laboured, therefore, with such goodwill, that he softened the breast of the Big Chief, who gradually became more amiable, and even indulgent to him. Thus he came to know experimentally the wisdom of that Scripture, "Be not overcome of evil, but overcome evil with good."

John Jarwin possessed a remarkably fine sonorous bass voice, which, in former days, had been a source of great delight to his messmates. Although strong and deep, it was very sweet and tender in its tones, and eminently suited for pathetic and sentimental songs. Indeed Jarwin's nature was so earnest, that although he had a great deal of quiet humour about him, and could enjoy comic songs very much, he never himself sang anything humorous. Now, it chanced that the Big Chief had a good ear for music, and soon became so fond of the songs which his slave was wont to hum when at work, that he used to make him sit down beside him frequently and sing for hours at a time! Fortunately, Jarwin's lungs were powerful, and his voice being full-toned and loud, he was able to sing as much as his master desired without much exertion. He gave him his whole budget which was pretty extensive—including melodies of the "Black-eyed Susan" and "Ben Bolt" stamp. When these had been sung over and over again, he took to the Psalms and Paraphrases—many of which he knew by heart, and, finally, he had recourse to extempore composition, which he found much easier than he had expected—the tones flowing naturally and the words being gibberish! Thus he became a sort of David to this remarkable Saul. By degrees, as he learnt the native tongue, he held long conversations with the Big Chief, and told him about his own land and countrymen and religion. In regard to the last the Chief was very inquisitive, and informed his slave that white men had been for some time in that region, trying to teach their religion to the men of an island which, though invisible from his island, was not very far distant. Jarwin said little about this, but from that time he began to hope that, through the missionaries, he might be able to make his escape ere long.

During all this time poor Cuffy experienced a variety of vicissitudes, and made several narrow escapes. At first he had been caught and was on the point of being killed and roasted, when he wriggled out of his captor's grasp and made off to the mountains, terrorstruck! Here he dwelt for some weeks in profound melancholy. Being unable to stand separation from his master any longer, he ventured to return to the village, but was immediately hunted out of it, and once again fled in horror to the hills. Jarwin was not allowed to quit the village alone, he therefore never saw his little dog, and at length came to the conclusion that it had been killed. When, however, he had ingratiated himself with his master, he was allowed more freedom, and one day, having wandered a considerable distance into the mountains, he came suddenly and unexpectedly upon Cuffy. Having experienced nothing from man of late but the most violent and cruel treatment, Cuffy no sooner beheld, as he supposed, one of his enemies, than, without giving him a second glance, he sprang up, put his ears back, his tail between his legs, and, uttering a terrible yell, fled "on the wings of terror!" But Jarwin put two fingers in his mouth and gave a peculiarly shrill whistle, which brought the dog to a sudden stop. He looked back with ears cocked. Again Jarwin whistled. Instantly Cuffy turned and ran at him with a series of mingled yells, whines, and barks, that gave but a faint idea of his tumultuous feelings. It would scarcely be too much to say that he almost ate his master up. He became like an india-rubber ball gone mad! He bounded round him to such an extent that Jarwin found it very difficult to get hold of or pat him. It is impossible to do justice to such a meeting. We draw a veil over it, only remarking that the sailor took his old favourite back to the village, and, after much entreaty and a good deal of persuasive song, was permitted to keep him.

About ten months after this event, war broke out between the Big Chief and a neighbouring tribe of natives, who were a very quarrelsome and vindictive set. The tribe with whom Jarwin dwelt would gladly have lived at peace, but the other tribe was stronger in numbers and thirsted for conquest—a consequence of strength which is by no means confined to savages!

When war was formally declared, the Big Chief told Jarwin to prepare himself for battle. At first our hero had some qualms of conscience about it, but on reflecting that on the part of the tribe to which he belonged it was a war of self-defence, his conscience was pacified.

The Big Chief ordered him to throw away his now ragged garments, smear his whole body over with oil and red earth, paint black spots on his cheeks, and a white streak down his nose, and put on warrior's costume. In vain Jarwin begged and protested and sang. The Big Chief's blood was up, and his commands must be obeyed, therefore Jarwin did as he was bid; went out to battle in this remarkable costume—if we may so style it—and proved himself such a prodigy of valour that his prowess went far to turn the tide of victory wherever he appeared during the fight. But we pass over all this. Suffice it to say, that the pugnacious tribe was severely chastised and reduced to a state of quiet—for the time at least.

One day, not long after the cessation of the war, a canoe arrived with several natives, all of whom wore clothing of a much more civilised description than is usually seen among South-Sea savages. They had a long, earnest talk with the natives, but Jarwin was not allowed to hear it, or to show himself. Next day they went away. For some time after that Big Chief was very thoughtful, but silent, and Jarwin could not induce him to become confidential until he had sung all his melodies and all his psalms several times over, and had indulged in extempore melody and gibberish until his brain and throat were alike exhausted. The Big Chief gave way at last, however, and told him that his late visitors were Christians, who, with two native teachers, had been sent from a distant island by a white chief named Williams, to try and persuade him and his people to burn their idols.

"And are 'ee goin' to do it?" asked Jarwin.

"No," replied the Chief, "but I am going to Raratonga to see Cookee Williams."

Of course they conversed in the native tongue, but as this would be unintelligible to the reader, we translate. It may also be remarked here that "Cookee" signified a white man, and is a word derived from the visit of that great navigator Captain Cook to these islands, by the natives of which he was ultimately murdered.

Jarwin had heard, while in England, of the missionary Williams. On learning that he was among the islands, his heart beat high, and he begged earnestly that he might be allowed to go with the chief and his party to Raratonga, but his wily master would not consent "You will run away!" he said.

"No, I won't," said Jarwin, earnestly. Big Chief shook his head. "They will take you from me," he said, "when they find out who you are."

"I'll not let 'em," replied Jarwin, with pathetic sincerity, and then began to sing in such a touching strain, that his master lay back on his couch and rolled his large eyes in rapture.

"You shall go, Jowin," (that was the best he could make of the name), "if you will make me a promise."

"Name it, old boy," said Jarwin.

"That you will go dressed like one of my young men, and never open your lips to speak a word, no more than if you were dumb, whether the Cookees speak to you or not."

Jarwin hesitated, but reflecting that there was no chance of his seeing the missionary at all if he did not give this promise, he consented.

A week after that all the preparations were made, and four large canoes, full of well-armed men, set out for Raratonga.

At the time we write of, the island of Raratonga had been recently discovered by the missionary Williams. The success of the labours of that devoted man and his native teachers, is one of the most marvellous chapters in the history of the isles of the Pacific. At Raratonga, God seemed to have prepared the way for the introduction of the Gospel in a wonderful manner, for although the native teachers who first went ashore there were roughly handled, they were enabled, nevertheless, to persevere, and in not much more than a single year, the Gospel wrought a change in the feelings and habits of the people, which was little short of miraculous. Within that brief period they had given up and burnt all their idols, had ceased to practise their bloody and horrible rites, and had embraced Christianity—giving full proof of their sincerity by submitting to a code of laws founded on Scripture, by agreeing to abandon polygamy, by building a large place of worship, and by leading comparatively virtuous and peaceful lives. And all this was begun and carried on for a considerable time, not by the European missionaries but by two of the devoted native teachers, who had previously embraced Christianity.

The extent of the change thus wrought in the Raratongans in so short a time by the Gospel, may be estimated by a glance at the difficulties with which the missionaries had to contend. In writing of the ancient usages of the people, Mr Williams, (See Williams' most interesting work, entitled "A Narrative of Missionary Enterprises in the South-Sea Islands"), tells us that one of their customs was an unnatural practice called *Kukumi anga*. As soon as a son reached manhood, he would fight and wrestle with his father for the mastery, and if he obtained it, would take forcible possession of the farm belonging to his parent, whom he drove in a state of destitution from his home. Another custom was equally unnatural and inhuman. When a woman lost her husband, the relatives of the latter, instead of paying visits of kindness to the fatherless and widow in their affliction, would seize every article of value belonging to the deceased, turn the disconsolate mother and her children away, and possess themselves of the house, food, and land. But they had another custom which caused still greater difficulties to the missionaries. It was called "land-eating"—in other words, the getting possession of each other's lands unjustly, and these, once obtained, were held with the greatest possible tenacity, for land was exceedingly valuable at Raratonga, and on no subject were the contentions of the people more frequent or fierce.

From this it will be seen that the Raratongans were apparently a most unpromising soil in which to plant the "good seed," for there is scarcely another race of people on earth so depraved and unnatural as they seem to have been. Nevertheless, God's blessed Word overcame these deep-rooted prejudices, and put an end to these and many other horrible practices in little more than a year.

After this glorious work had been accomplished, the energetic missionary—who ultimately laid down his life in one of these islands (*The Island of Erramanga*) for the sake of Jesus Christ—resolved to go himself in search of other islands in which to plant the Gospel, and to send out native teachers with the same end in view. The record of their labours reads more like a romance than a reality, but we cannot afford to diverge longer from the course of our narrative. It was one of these searching parties of native teachers that had visited the Big Chief's island as already described, and it was their glowing words and representations that had induced him to undertake this voyage to Raratonga.

Big Chief of course occupied the largest of the four canoes, and our friend Jarwin sat on a seat in front of him—painted and decorated like a native warrior, and wielding a paddle like the rest. Of course Cuffy had been left behind.

Poor Jarwin had, during his captivity, undergone the process of being tatooed from head to foot. It had taken several months to accomplish and had cost him inexpressible torture, owing to the innumerable punctures made by the comb-like instrument with which it was done on the inflamed muscles of his body. By dint of earnest entreaty and much song, he had prevailed on Big Chief to leave his face and hands untouched. It is doubtful if he would have succeeded in this, despite the witching power of his melodious voice, had he not at the same time offered to paint his own face in imitation of tatooing, and accomplished the feat to such perfection that his delighted master insisted on having his own painted forthwith in the same style.

During a pause in their progress, while the paddlers were resting, Big Chief made his captive sit near him.

"You tell me that Cookee-men" (by which he meant white men) "never lie, never deceive."

"I shud lie an' deceive myself, if I said so," replied Jarwin, bluntly.

"What did you tell me, then?" asked the Chief, with a frown.

"I told you that *Christian* men don't lie or deceive—leastwise they don't do it with a will."

"Are *you* a Christian man, Jowin?"

"I am," replied the sailor promptly. Then with a somewhat perplexed air, "Anyhow I *hope* I am, an' I try to act as sitch."

"Good, I will soon prove it. You will be near the Cookee-men of Raratonga to-morrow. You will have chance to go with them and leave me; but if you do, or if you speak one word of Cookee-tongue—you are *not* Christian. Moreover, I will batter your skull with my club, till it is like the soft pulp of the bread-fruit."

"You're a cute fellar, as the Yankees say," remarked Jarwin, with a slight smile. This being said in English, the Chief took no notice of it, but glanced at his slave suspiciously.

"Big Chief," said Jarwin, after a short silence, "even before I was a Christian, I had been taught by my mother to be ashamed of telling a lie, so you've no occasion for to doubt me. But it's a hard thing to stand by a countryman, specially in my pecooliar circumstances, an' not let him know that you can speak to him. May I not be allowed to palaver a bit with 'em? I wont ask 'em to take me from you."

"No," said the Chief sternly. "You came with me promising that you would not even speak to the Cookee-men."

"Well, Big Chief," replied Jarwin, energetically, "you shall see that a British seaman can stick to his promise. I'll be true to you. Honour bright. I'll not give 'em a word of the English lingo if they was to try to tear it out o' me wi' red hot pincers. I'll content myself wi' lookin' at 'em and listenin' to 'em. It'll be a comfort to hear my mother-tongue, anyhow."

"Good," replied the Chief, "I trust you."

The interval of rest coming to an end at this point, the conversation ceased and the paddles were resumed.

It was a magnificent day. The great Pacific was in that condition of perfect repose which its name suggests. Not a breath of air ruffled the wide sheet of water, which lay spread out like a vast circular looking-glass to reflect the sky, and it did reflect the sky with such perfect fidelity, that the clouds and cloudlets in the deep were exact counterparts of those that floated in the air, while the four canoes, resting on their own reflections, seemed to be suspended in the centre of a crystal world, which was dazzlingly lit up by two resplendent suns.

This condition of calm lasted the whole of that day and night, and the heat was very great; nevertheless the warriors—of whom there were from forty to fifty in each canoe—did not cease to paddle for an instant, save when the short spells of rest came round, and when, twice during the day, they stopped to eat a hasty meal.

When the sun set they still continued to paddle onwards, the only difference being that instead of passing over a sea of crystal, they appeared to traverse an ocean of amber and burnished gold. All night they continued their labours. About daybreak the Chief permitted them to enjoy a somewhat longer period of rest, during which most of them, without lying down, indulged in a short but refreshing nap. Resuming the paddles, they proceeded until sunrise, when their hearts were gladdened by the sight of the blue hills of Raratonga on the bright horizon.

"Now we shall soon be at the end of our voyage," said the Chief, as he pointed to the distant hills, and glanced at Jarwin as he might at a prize which he was much afraid of losing. "Remember the promise, you Christian. Don't be a deceiver, you 'Breetish tar!'" (He quoted Jarwin here.)

"Honour bright!" replied our hero.

The savage gazed earnestly into the sailor's bright eyes, and appeared to think that if his honour was as bright as they were, there was not much cause to fear. At all events he looked pleased, nodded his head, and said "Good," with considerable emphasis.

By this time the hills of Raratonga were beginning to look less like blue clouds and more like real mountains; gradually as the canoes drew nearer, the markings on them became more and more defined, until at last everything was distinctly visible—rocky eminences and luxuriant valleys, through which flowed streams and rivulets that glittered brightly in the light of the ascending sun, and almost constrained Jarwin to shout with delight, for he gazed upon a scene more lovely by far than anything that he had yet beheld in the Southern Seas.

Chapter Seven

Our Hero is Exposed to Stirring Influences and Trying Circumstances

When the four canoes drew near to the island, immense numbers of natives were seen to assemble on the beach, so that Big Chief deemed it advisable to advance with caution. Presently a solitary figure, either dressed or painted black, advanced in front of the others and waved a white flag. This seemed to increase the Chief's anxiety, for he ordered the men to cease paddling.

Jarwin, whose heart had leaped with delight when he saw the dark figure and the white flag, immediately turned round and said—

"You needn't be afraid, old boy; that's the missionary, I'll be bound, in his black toggery, an' a white flag means 'peace' among Cookee men."

On hearing this, the Chief gave the order to advance, and Jarwin, seizing a piece of native cloth that lay near him, waved it round his head.

"Stop that, you Breetish tar!" growled Big Chief, seizing a huge club, which bristled with shark's teeth, and shaking it at the seaman, while his own teeth were displayed in a threatening grin.

"All right, old codger," replied the British tar, with a submissive look; "honour bright, honour bright," he added several times, in a low tone, as if to keep himself in mind of his promise.

We have already said that our hero and his master talked in the native tongue, which the former had acquired with wonderful facility, but such familiar expressions as "old boy," "old codger," etcetera, were necessarily uttered in English. Fortunately for Jarwin, who was by nature free-and-easy, the savage chief imagined these to be terms of respect, and was, consequently, rather pleased to hear them. Similarly, Big Chief said "Breetish tar" and "Christian" in English, as he had learned them from his captive. When master and slave began to grow fond of each other—as we have seen that they soon did, their manly natures being congenial—they used these expressions more frequently: Jarwin meaning to express facetious goodwill, but his master desiring to express kindly regard, except when he was roused to anger, in which case he did not, however, use them contemptuously, but as expressive of earnest solemnity.

On landing, Big Chief and his warriors were received by the Reverend Mr Williams and his native teachers—of whom there were two men and two women—with every demonstration of kindness, and were informed that the island of Raratonga had cast away and burned its idols, and now worshipped the true God, who had sent His Son Jesus Christ to save the world from sin.

"I know that," replied Big Chief to the teacher who interpreted; "converts, like yourself, came to my island not long ago, and told me all about it. Now I have come to see and hear. A wise man will know and understand before he acts."

Big Chief was then conducted to the presence of the king of that part of the island, who stood, surrounded by his chief men, under a grove of Temanu trees. The king, whose name was Makea, was a handsome man, in the prime of life, about six feet high, and very massive and muscular. He had a noble appearance and commanding aspect, and, though not so tall as Big Chief, was, obviously, a man of superior power in every way. His complexion was light, and his body most beautifully tatooed and slightly coloured with a preparation of tumeric and ginger, which gave it a light orange tinge, and, in the estimation of the Raratongans, added much to the beauty of his appearance.

The two chiefs advanced frankly to each other, and amiably rubbed noses together—the South Sea method of salutation! Then a long palaver ensued, in which Big Chief explained the object of his visit, namely, to hear about the new religion, and to witness its effects with his own eyes. The missionary gladly gave him a full account of all he desired to know, and earnestly urged him to accept the Gospel of Jesus Christ, and to throw away his idols.

Big Chief and his men listened with earnest attention and intense gravity, and, after the palaver was over, retired to consult together in private.

During all this time poor Jarwin's heart had been greatly stirred. Being tatooed, and nearly naked, as well as painted like the rest of his comrades, of course no one took particular notice of him, which depressed him greatly, for he felt an intense desire to seize the missionary by the hand, and claim him as a countryman. Indeed this feeling was so strong upon him on first hearing Mr Williams's English tone of voice—although the missionary spoke only in the native tongue—that he could scarcely restrain himself, and had to mutter "honour bright" several times, in order, as it were, to hold himself in check. "Honour bright" became his moral rein, or curb, on that trying occasion. But when, in the course of the palaver, Mrs Williams, who had accompanied her husband on this dangerous expedition, came forward and addressed a few words to the missionary in English, he involuntarily sprang forward with an exclamation of delight at hearing once more the old familiar tongue. He glanced, however, at Big Chief, and checked himself. There was a stern expression on the brow of the savage, but his eyes remained fixed on the ground, and his form and face were immovable, as though he heard and saw nothing.

"Honour bright," whispered Jarwin, as he turned about and retired among his comrades.

Fortunately his sudden action had only attracted the attention of a few of those who were nearest to him, and no notice was taken of it.

When Big Chief retired with his men for consultation, he called Jarwin aside.

"Jarwin," he said, with unusual gravity, "you must not hear our palaver."

"Why not, old feller?"

"It is your business to obey, not to question," replied Big Chief, sternly. "Go—when I want you I will find you. You may go and *look* at the Cookee missionary, but, remember, I have your promise."

"Honour bright," replied Jarwin with a sigh.

"The promise of a Breetish tar?"

"Surely," replied Jarwin.

"Of a *Christian*?" said Big Chief, with emphasis.

"Aye, that's the idee; but it's a hard case, old boy, to advise a poor feller to go into the very jaws o' temptation. I would rather 'ee had ordered me to keep away from 'em. Howsever, here goes!"

Muttering these words to himself, he left his savage friends to hold their palaver, and went straight into the "jaws of temptation," by walking towards the cottage of the missionary. It was a neat wooden erection, built and plastered by the natives. Jarwin hung about the door; sometimes he even ventured to peep in at the windows, in his intense desire to see and hear the long-lost forms and tones of his native land; and, as the natives generally were much addicted to such indications of curiosity, his doing so attracted no unusual attention.

While he was standing near the door, Mrs Williams unexpectedly came out. Jarwin, feeling ashamed to appear in so *very* light a costume before a lady, turned smartly round and walked away. Then, reflecting that he was quite as decently clothed as the other natives about, he turned again and slowly retraced his steps, pretending to be interested in picking stones and plants from the ground.

The missionary's wife looked at him for a moment with no greater interest than she would have bestowed on any other native, and then gazed towards the sea-shore, as if she expected some one. Presently Mr Williams approached.

"Well, have you been successful?" she asked.

"Yes, it has been all arranged satisfactorily, so I shall begin at once," replied Mr Williams. "The only thing that gives me anxiety is the bellows."

Poor Jarwin drew nearer and nearer. His heart was again stirred in a way that it had not been for many a day, and he had to pull the rein pretty tightly; in fact, it required all his Christianity and British-tar-hood to prevent him from revealing himself, and claiming protection at that moment.

As he raised himself, and gazed with intense interest at the speakers, the missionary's attention became fixed on him, and he beckoned him to approach.

"I think you are one of the strangers who have just arrived, are you not?"

This was spoken in the language of Raratonga, which was so similar to that which he had already acquired, that he opened his mouth to reply, "Yes, your honour," or "Your reverence," in English. But it suddenly occurred to him that he must translate this into the native tongue if his secret was to be preserved. While he was turning over in his mind the best words to use for this purpose he reflected that the imperfection of his knowledge, even the mere tone of his voice, would probably betray him; he therefore remained dumb, with his mouth open.

The missionary smiled slightly, and repeated his question.

Jarwin, in great perplexity, still remained dumb. Suddenly an idea flashed across his mind. He pointed to his mouth, wagged his tongue, and shook his head.

"Ah! you are dumb, my poor man," said the missionary, with a look of pity.

"Or tabooed," suggested the lady; "his tongue may have been tabooed."

There was some reason and probability in this, for the extraordinary custom of tabooing, by which various things are supposed to be rendered sacred, and therefore not to be used or touched, is extended by the South Sea Islanders to various parts of their bodies, as for instance, the hands; in which case the person so tabooed must, for a time, be fed by others, as he dare not use his hands.

Jarwin, being aware of the custom, was so tickled by the idea of his tongue being tabooed, that he burst into an uncontrollable fit of laughter, to the intense amazement of his questioners. While in the midst of this laugh, he became horrified by the thought that *that* of itself would be sufficient to betray him, so he cleverly remedied the evil, and gave vent to his feelings by tapering the laugh off into a hideous yell, and rushed frantically from the spot.

"Strange," observed the missionary, gazing after the fugitive mariner, "how like that was to an English laugh!"

"More like the cry of a South Sea maniac, I think," said Mrs Williams, re-entering the house, followed by her husband.

The matter which the missionary said had been arranged so satisfactorily, and was to be begun at once, was neither more nor less than the building of a ship, in which to traverse the great island-studded breast of the Pacific.

In case some one, accustomed to think of the ponderous vessels which are built constantly in this land with such speed and facility, should be inclined to regard the building of a ship a small matter, we shall point out a few of the difficulties with which the missionary had to contend in this projected work.

In the first place, he was on what is sometimes styled a "savage island"—an island that lay far out of the usual track of ships, that had only been discovered a little more than a year at that time, and was inhabited by a blood-thirsty, savage, cruel, and ignorant race of human beings, who had renounced idolatry and embraced Christianity only a few months before. They knew no more of ship-building than the celebrated man in the moon, and their methods of building canoes were quite inapplicable to vessels of large capacity. Besides this, Mr Williams was the only white man on the island, and he had no suitable implements for shipbuilding, except axes and augurs, and a few of the smaller of the carpenter's tools. In the building of a vessel, timbers and planks are indispensable, but he had no pit-saw wherewith to cut these. It is necessary to fasten planks and timbers together, but he had no nails to do this. Heavy iron forgings were required for some parts of the structure, but, although he possessed iron, he had no smith's anvil, or hammer, or tongs, or bellows, wherewith to forge it. In these circumstances he commenced one of the greatest pieces of work ever undertaken by man—greatest, not only because of the mechanical difficulties overcome, but because of the influence for good that the ship, when completed, had upon the natives of the Southern Seas, as well as its reflex influence in exciting admiration, emulation, and enthusiasm in other lands.

The first difficulty was the bellows. Nothing could be done without these and the forge. There were four goats on the island. Three of these were sacrificed; their skins were cut up, and, along with two boards, converted into a pair of smith's bellows in four days.

No one can imagine the intense interest with which John Jarwin looked on while the persevering but inexperienced missionary laboured at this work, and tremendous was the struggle which he had to keep his hands idle and his tongue quiet; for he was a mechanical genius, and could have given the missionary many a useful hint, but did not dare to do so lest his knowledge, or voice, or aptitude for such work, or all these put together, should betray him. He was, therefore, fain to content himself with looking on, or performing a few trifling acts in the way of lifting, carrying, and hewing with the axe.

His friends frequently came to look on, as the work progressed, and he could not help fancying that they regarded him with looks of peculiar interest. This perplexed him, but, supposing that it must result from suspicion of his integrity, he took no notice of it, save that he became more resolute than ever in reference to "honour bright!" Big Chief also came to look on and wonder, but, although he kept a sharp eye on his slave, he did not seem to desire intercourse with him.

When the bellows were finished, it was found that they did not work properly. The upper box did not fill well, and, when tried, they were not satisfied with blowing wind out, but insisted on drawing fire in! They were, in short, a failure! Deep were the ponderings of the missionary as to how this was to be remedied, and small was the light thrown on the subject by the various encyclopaedias and other books which he possessed; but the question was somewhat abruptly settled for him by the rats. These creatures devoured all the leather of the bellows in a single night, and left nothing but the bare boards!

Rats were an absolute plague at that time at Raratonga. Mr Williams tells us, in his interesting "Narrative," that he and his family never sat down to a meal without having two or more persons stationed to keep them off the table. When kneeling at family prayer, they would run over them in all directions, and it was found difficult to keep them out of the beds. On one occasion, when the servant was making one of the beds, she uttered a scream, and, on rushing into the room, Mr Williams found that four rats had crept under the pillow and made themselves snug there. They paid for their impudence, however, with their lives. On another occasion, a pair of English shoes, which had not been put in the usual place of safety, were totally devoured in a night, and the same fate befell the covering of a hair-trunk. No wonder, then, that they did not spare the bellows!

Poor Jarwin sorrowed over this loss fully as much as did the missionary, but he was forced to conceal his grief.

Still bent on discovering some method of "raising the wind," Mr Williams appealed to his inventive powers. He considered that if a pump threw water, there was no reason why it should not throw wind. Impressed with this belief, he set to work and made a box about eighteen or twenty inches square and four feet high, with a valve in the bottom to let air in, a hole in the front to let it out, and a sort of piston to force it through the hole. By means of a long lever the piston could be raised, and by heavy weights it was pushed down. Of course considerable power was required to raise the piston and its weights, but there was a superabundance of power, for thousands of wondering natives were ready and eager to do whatever they were bid. They could have pumped the bellows had they been the size of a house! They worked admirably in some respects, but had the same fault as the first pair, namely, a tendency to suck in the fire! This, however, was corrected by means of a valve at the back of the pipe which communicated with the fire. Another fault lay in the length of interval between the blasts. This was remedied by making another box of the same kind, and working the two alternately, so that when one was blowing the fire, the other was, as it were, taking breath. Thus a continuous blast was obtained, while eight or ten grinning and delighted natives worked the levers.

The great difficulty being thus overcome, the work progressed rapidly. A large hard stone served for an anvil, and a small stone, perforated, with a handle affixed to it, did duty for a hammer. A pair of carpenter's pincers served for tongs, and charcoal, made from the cocoanut and other trees, did duty for coals. In order to obtain planks, the missionary split trees in half with wedges and then the natives thinned them down with adzes extemporised by fitting crooked handles to ordinary hatchets. When a bent or twisted plank was required, having no apparatus for steaming it, he bent a piece of bamboo to the required shape, and sent natives to scour the woods in search of a suitable crooked tree. Thus planks suited to his purpose were obtained. Instead of fastening the planks to the timbers of the ship with iron nails, large wooden pins, or "trenails," were used, and driven into augur holes, and thus the fabric was held together. Instead of oakum, cocoanut husk was used, and native cloth and dried banana stumps to caulk the seams, and make them watertight. The bark of a certain tree was spun into twine and rope by a rope-machine made for the purpose, and a still more complex machine, namely, a turning-lathe, was constructed for the purpose of turning the block sheaves; while sails were made out of native mats, quilted to give them sufficient strength to resist the wind.

By these means was completed, in about three months, a decked vessel of from seventy to eighty tons burden—about sixty feet long by eighteen broad. She was finally launched and named *The Messenger of Peace*. And, truly, a messenger of peace and glad tidings did she afterwards prove to be on many occasions among the islands of the Southern Seas.

But our hero, John Jarwin, was not allowed to remain to see this happy consummation. He only looked on and assisted at the commencement of the work.

Many and many a time did he, during that trying period, argue with himself as to the propriety of his conduct in thus refusing the means of escape when it was thrown in his way, and there was not wanting, now and then, a suggestion from somewhere—he knew not where, but certainly it was not from outside of him—that perhaps the opportunity had been *providentially* thrown in his way. But Jarwin resisted these suggestions. He looked *up*, and reflected that he was there under a solemn promise; that, but for his promise, he should not have been there at all, and that, therefore, it was his peculiar duty at that particular time to whisper to himself continually—"honour bright!"

One morning Big Chief roused Jarwin with his toe, and said—

"Get up. We go home now."

"What say 'ee, old man?"

"Get ready. We go to-day. I have seen and heard enough."

Big Chief was very stern, so that Jarwin thought it wise to hold his tongue and obey.

There was a long animated palaver between the chief, the missionary, and the king, but Jarwin had been carefully prevented from hearing it by his master, who ordered him to keep by the canoes, which were launched and ready. Once again he was assailed by an intense desire to escape, and this sudden approach of the time that was perchance to fix his fate for life rendered him almost desperate—but he still looked up, and "honour bright" carried the day. He remained dumb to the last, and did not even allow himself the small comfort of waving a piece of native cloth to the missionary, as he and his captors paddled from the Raratonga shore.

Chapter Eight

Despair is Followed by Surprises and Deliverance

At first John Jarwin could not quite realise his true position after leaving Raratonga. The excitement consequent on the whole affair remained for some time on his mind, causing him to feel as if it were a dream, and it was not until he had fairly landed again on Big Chief's island, and returned to his own little hut there, and had met with Cuffy—whose demonstrations of intense delight cannot by any possibility be described—that he came fully to understand the value of the opportunity which he had let slip through his fingers.

Poor Jarwin! words fail to convey a correct idea of the depth of his despair, for now he saw clearly, as he thought, that perpetual slavery was his doom. Under the influence of the feelings that overwhelmed him he became savage.

"Cuff," said he, on the afternoon of the day of his return, "it's all up with you and me, old chap."

The tone in which this was uttered was so stern that the terrier drooped its ears, lowered its tail, and looked up with an expression that was equivalent to "Don't kick me, *please* don't!"

Jarwin smiled a grim yet a pitiful smile as he looked at the dog.

"Yes, it's all up with us," he continued; "we shall live and die in slavery; wot a fool I was not to cut and run when I had the chance!"

The remembrance of "honour bright" flashed upon him here, but he was still savage, and therefore doggedly shut his eyes to it.

At this point a message was brought to him from Big Chief requesting his attendance in the royal hut. Jarwin turned angrily on the messenger and bid him begone in a voice of thunder, at the same time intimating, by a motion of his foot, that if he did not obey smartly, he would quicken his motions for him. The messenger vanished, and Jarwin sat down beside Cuffy—who looked excessively humble—and vented his feelings thus—

"I can't stand it no longer Cuff. I *won't* stand it! I'm goin' to bust up, I am; so look out for squalls."

A feeling of uncertainty as to the best method of "busting up" induced him to clutch his hair with both hands, and snort. It must not be supposed that our hero gave way to such rebellious feelings with impunity. On the contrary, his conscience pricked him to such an extent that it felt like an internal pin-cushion or hedgehog. While he was still holding fast to his locks in meditative uncertainty, three natives appeared at the entrance of his hut, and announced that they had been sent by Big Chief to take him to the royal hut by force, in case he should refuse to go peaceably.

Uttering a shout of defiance, the exasperated man sprang up and rushed at the natives, who, much too wise to await the onset, fled in three different directions. Instead of pursuing any of them, Jarwin went straight to his master's hut, where he found him seated on a couch of native cloth. Striding up to him he clenched his fist, and holding it up in a threatening manner, exclaimed—

"Now look 'ee here, Big Chief—which it would be big thief if 'ee had yer right name—I ain't goin' to stand this sort o' thing no longer. I kep' my word to you all the time we wos at Raratonga, but now I'll keep it no longer. I'll do my best to cut the cable and make sail the wery first chance I gits—so I give 'ee fair warnin'."

Big Chief made no reply for some moments, but opened his eyes with such an intense expression of unaffected amazement, that Jarwin's wrath abated, in spite of his careful nursing of it to keep it warm.

"Jowin," he exclaimed at length, "you Christian Breetish tar, have your dibbil got into you?"

This question effectually routed Jarwin's anger. He knew that the savage, to whom he had spoken at various times on the subject of satanic influence, was perfectly sincere in his inquiry, as well as in his astonishment. Moreover, he himself felt surprised that Big Chief, who was noted for his readiness to resent insult, should have submitted to his angry tones and looks and threatening manner without the slightest evidence of indignation. The two men therefore stood looking at each other in silent surprise for a few moments.

"Big Chief," said Jarwin at last, bringing his right fist down heavily into his left palm, by way of emphasis, "there's no dibbil, as you call him, got possession o' me. My own spirit is dibbil enough, I find, to account for all that I've said and done—an' a great deal more. But it *has* bin hard on me to see the door open, as it were, an' not take adwantage of it. Howsever, it's all over now, an' I ax yer parding. I'll not mutiny again. You've been a kind feller to me, old chap—though you *are* a savage—an' I ain't on-grateful; as long as I'm your slave I'll do my duty—'honour bright;' at the same time I think it fair an' above board to let you know that I'll make my escape from you when I git the chance. I'm bound for to sarve you while I eat your wittles, but I am free to go if I can manage it. There—you may roast me alive an' eat me, if you like, but you can't say, after this, that I'm sailin' under false colours."

During this speech a variety of expressions affected the countenance of Big Chief, but that of melancholy predominated.

"Jowin," he said, slowly, "I like you."

"You're a good-hearted old buffer," said Jarwin, grasping the Chief's hand, and squeezing it; "to say the truth, I'm wery fond o' yourself, but it's nat'ral that I should like my freedom better."

Big Chief pondered this for some time, and shook his head slowly, as if the result of his meditation was not satisfactory.

"Jowin," he resumed, after a pause, "sing me a song."

"Well, you *are* a queer codger," said Jarwin, laughing in spite of himself; "if ever there was a man as didn't feel up to singin', that's me at this moment. Howsomedever, I 'spose it must be done. Wot'll you 'ave? 'Ben Bolt,' 'Black-eyed Susan,' 'The Jolly Young Waterman,' 'Jim Crow,' 'There is a Happy Land,' or the 'Old Hundred,' eh? Only say the word, an' I'll turn on the steam."

Big Chief made no reply. As he appeared to be lost in meditation, Jarwin sat down, and in a species of desperation, began to bellow with all the strength of his lungs one of those nautical ditties with which seamen are wont to enliven the movements of the windlass or the capstan. He changed the tune several times, and at length slid gradually into a more gentle and melodious vein of song, while Big Chief listened with evident pleasure. Still there was perceptible to Jarwin a dash of sadness in his master's countenance which he had never seen before. Wondering at this, and changing his tunes to suit his own varying moods, he gradually came to plaintive songs, and then to psalms and hymns.

At last Big Chief seemed satisfied, and bade his slave good-night.

"He's a wonderful c'racter," remarked Jarwin to Cuffy, as he lay down to rest that night, "a most onaccountable sort o' man. There's sumthin' workin' in 'is 'ead; tho' wot it may be is more nor I can tell. P'raps he's agoin' to spiflicate me, in consikence o' my impidence. If so, Cuff, whatever will became o' you, my poor little doggie!"

Cuffy nestled very close to his master's side at this point, and whined in a pitiful tone, as if he really understood the purport of his remarks. In five minutes more he was giving vent to occasional mild little whines and half barks, indicating that he was in the land of dreams, and Jarwin's nose was creating sounds which told that its owner had reached that blessed asylum of the weary—oblivion.

Next day our sailor awakened to the consciousness of the fact that the sun was shining brightly, that paroquets were chattering gaily, that Cuffy was still sleeping soundly, and that the subjects of Big Chief were making an unusual uproar outside.

Starting up, and pulling on a pair of remarkably ancient canvas trousers, which his master had graciously permitted him to retain and wear, Jarwin looked out at the door of his hut and became aware of the fact that the whole tribe was assembled in the spot where national "palavers" were wont to be held. The "House" appeared to be engaged at the time in the discussion of some exceedingly knotty question—a sort of national education bill, or church endowment scheme—for there was great excitement, much gesticulation, and very loud talk, accompanied with not a little angry demonstration on the part of the disputants.

"Hallo! wot's up?" inquired Jarwin of a stout savage who stood at his door armed with a club, on the head of which human teeth formed a conspicuous ornament.

"Palaver," replied the savage.

"It's easy to hear and see that," replied Jarwin, "but wot is it all about?"

The savage vouchsafed no farther reply, but continued to march up and down in front of the hut.

Jarwin, therefore, essayed to quit his abode, but was stopped by the taciturn savage, who said that he must consider himself a prisoner until the palaver had come to an end. He was therefore fain to content himself with standing at his door and watching the gesticulations of the members of council.

Big Chief was there of course, and appeared to take a prominent part in the proceedings. But there were other chiefs of the tribe whose opinions had much weight, though they were inferior to him in position. At last they appeared to agree, and finally, with a loud shout, the whole band rushed off in the direction of the temple where their idols were kept.

Jarwin's guard had manifested intense excitement during the closing scene, and when this last act took place he threw down his club, forsook his post, and followed his comrades. Of course Jarwin availed himself of the opportunity, and went to see what was being done.

To his great surprise he found that the temple was being dismantled, while the idols were carried down to the palaver-ground, if we may so call it, and thrown into a heap there with marks of indignity and contempt.

Knowing, as he did, the superstitious reverence with which the natives regarded their idols, Jarwin beheld this state of things with intense amazement, and he looked on with increasing interest, hoping, ere long, to discover some clue to the mystery, but his hopes were disappointed, for Big Chief caught sight of him and sternly ordered him back to his hut, where another guard was placed over him. This guard was more strict than the previous one had been. He would not allow his prisoner even to look on at what was taking place.

Under the circumstances, there was therefore nothing for it but to fall back on philosophic meditation and converse with Cuffy. These were rather poor resources, however, to a man who was surrounded by a tribe of excited savages. Despite his natural courage and coolness, Jarwin felt, as he said himself, "raither oncomfortable."

Towards the afternoon things became a little more quiet, still no notice was taken of our hero save that his meals were sent to him from the Chief's hut. He wondered at this greatly, for nothing of the kind had ever happened before, and he began to entertain vague suspicions that such treatment might possibly be the prelude to evil of some kind befalling him. He questioned his guard several times, but that functionary told him that Big Chief had bidden him refuse to hold converse with him on any subject whatever.

Being, as the reader knows, a practical, matter-of-fact sort of man, our hero at last resigned himself to his fate, whatever that might be, and beguiled the time by making many shrewd remarks and observations to Cuffy. When the afternoon meal was brought to him, he heaved a deep sigh, and apparently, with that effort flung off all his anxieties.

"Come along, Cuff," he said in a hearty voice, sitting down to dinner, "let's grub together an' be thankful for small mercies, anyhow. Wotever turns up, you and I shall go halves and stick by one another to the last. Not that I have any doubts of Big Chief, Cuffy; you mustn't suppose that; but then, you see, he ain't the only chief in the island, and if all the rest was to go agin him, *he* couldn't do much to save us."

The dog of course replied in its usual facetious manner with eyes and tail, and sat down with its ears cocked and its head turned expectantly on one side, while the sailor removed the palm-leaf covering of the basket which contained the provisions sent to him.

"Wot have we here, Cuffy?" he said soliloquising and looking earnestly in; "let me see; bit of baked pig—good, Cuff, good; that's the stuff to make us fat. Wot next? Roast fish—that's not bad, Cuff—not bad, though hardly equal to the pig. Here we have a leaf full of plantains and another of yams,—excellent grub that, my doggie, nothing could be better. What's this? Cocoanut full of its own milk—the best o' drink; 'it cheers'—as the old song, or the old poet says—'but it don't inebriate;' that wos said in regard to tea, you know, but it holds good in respect of cocoanut milk, and it's far better than grog, Cuffy; far better, though you can't know nothin' about that, but you may take my word for it; happy is the man as drinks nothin' stronger than cocoanut milk or tea. Hallo! wot's this—plums? Why, doggie, they're oncommon good to us to-day. I wonder wot's up. I say—" Jarwin paused as he drew the last dish out of the prolific basket, and looked earnestly at his dog while he laid it down, "I say, what if they should have taken it into their heads to fatten us up before killin' us? That's not a wery agreeable notion, is it, eh?"

Apparently Cuffy was of the same opinion, for he did not wag even the point of his tail, and there was something dubious in the glance of his eye as he waited for more.

"Well, well, it ain't no use surmisin'," observed the seaman, with another sigh, "wot we've got for to do just now is to eat our wittles an' hope for the best. Here you are, Cuff—catch!"

Throwing a lump of baked pig to his dog, the worthy man fell to with a keen appetite, and gave himself no further anxiety as to the probable or possible events of the future.

Dinner concluded, he would fain have gone out for a ramble on the shore—as he had been wont to do in time past—but his gaoler forbade him to quit the hut. He was therefore about to console himself with a siesta, when an unexpected order came from Big Chief, requiring his immediate attendance in the royal hut. Jarwin at once obeyed the mandate, and in a few minutes stood before his master, who was seated on a raised couch, enjoying a cup of cocoanut milk.

"I have send for you," began Big Chief with solemnity, "to have a palaver. Sit down, you Breetish tar."

"All right, old chap," replied Jarwin, seating himself on a stool opposite to his master. "Wot is it to be about?"

"Jowin," rejoined Big Chief, with deepening gravity, "you's bin well treated here."

Big Chief spoke in broken English now, having picked it up with amazing facility from his white slave.

"Well, y–e–es, I'm free to confess that I *has* bin well treated—barrin' the fact that my liberty's bin took away; besides which, some of your black rascals ain't quite so civil as they might be, but on the whole, I've been well treated; anyhow I never received nothin' but kindness from *you*, old codger."

He extended his hand frankly, and Big Chief, who had been taught the meaning of our English method of salutation, grasped it warmly and shook it with such vigour that he would certainly have discomposed Jarwin had that "Breetish tar" been a less powerful man. He performed this ceremony with the utmost sadness, however, and continued to shake his head in such a melancholy way that his white slave began to feel quite anxious about him.

"Hallo! old feller, you ain't bin took bad, have 'ee?"

Big Chief made no reply, but continued to shake his head slowly; then, as if a sudden idea had occurred to him, he rose, and, grasping Jarwin by his whiskers with both hands, rubbed noses with him, after which he resumed his seat on the couch.

"Just so," observed our hero with a smile, "you shake hands with me English fashion—I rub noses with you South-Sea fashion. Give an' take; all right, old codger—'may our friendship last for ever,' as the old song puts it. But wot about this here palaver you spoke of? It warn't merely to rub our beaks together that you sent for me, I fancy. Is it a song you wants, or a hymn? Only say the word, and I'm your man."

"I s'pose," said Big Chief, using, of course, Jarwin's sea phraseology, only still farther broken, "you'd up ankar an' make sail most quick if you could, eh?"

"Well, although I *has* a likin' for you, old man," replied the sailor, "I can't but feel a sort o' preference, d'ee see, for my own wife an' child'n. There*fore* I *would* cut my cable, if I had the chance."

"Kite right, kite right," replied Big Chief, with a deep sigh, "you say it am nat'ral. Good, good, so 'tis. Now, Jowin," continued the savage chief, with intense earnestness, "you's free to go when you pleases."

"Oh, gammon!" replied Jarwin, with an unbelieving grin.

"Wot *is* gammon?" demanded Big Chief, with a somewhat disappointed look.

"Well, it don't matter what it means—it's nothin' or nonsense, if you like—but wot do *you* mean, old man, 'that's the rub,' as Hamblet, or some such c'racter, said to his father-in-law; you ain't in airnest, are you?"

"Jowin," answered the Chief, with immovable gravity, "I not onderstan' you. Wot you mean by airnest?" He did not wait for a reply, however, but seizing Jarwin by the wrist, and looking into his eyes with an expression of child-like earnestness that effectually solemnised his white slave, continued, "Lissen, onderstan' me. I is a Christian. My broder chiefs an' I have watch you many days. You have always do wot is right, no matter wot trouble follers to you. You do this for love of your God, your Saviour, so you tells me. Good, I do not need much palaver. Wen de sun shines it am hot; wen not shine am cold. Wot more? Cookee missionary have *say* the truth. My slave have *prove* the truth. I love you, Jowin. I love your God. I keep you if possible, but Christian must not have slave. Go—you is free."

"You don't mean *that*, old man?" cried Jarwin, starting up with flashing eyes and seizing his master's hand.

"You is free!" repeated Big Chief.

We need not relate all that honest John Jarwin said and did after that. Let it suffice to record his closing remarks that night to Cuffy.

"Cuff," said he, patting the shaggy head of his humble friend, "many a strange thing crops up in this here koorious world, but it never did occur to my mind before, that while a larned man like a missionary might *state* the truth, the likes o' me should have the chance an' the power to *prove* it. That's a wery koorious fact, so you an' I shall go to sleep on it, my doggie—good-night."

Chapter Nine

The Last

That Jarwin's deliverance from slavery was not a dream, but a blessed reality, was proved to him next day beyond all doubt by the singular proceedings of Big Chief and his tribe. Such of the native idols as had not been burned on the previous day were brought out, collected into a heap, and publicly burned, after which the whole tribe assembled on the palavering ground, and Big Chief made a long, earnest, and animated speech, in which he related all that he had seen of his white slave's conduct at the island of Raratonga, and stated how that conduct had proved to him, more conclusively than anything else he had heard or seen, that the religion of the white missionaries was true.

While this was being spoken, many sage reflections were passing through Jarwin's mind, and a feeling of solemn thankfulness filled him when he remembered how narrowly he had escaped doing inconceivable damage by giving way to temptation and breaking his word. He could not avoid perceiving that, if he had not been preserved in a course of rectitude all through his terrible trial, at a time when he thought that no one was thinking about him, not only would Big Chief and his nation have probably remained in heathen superstition, and continued to practise all the horrid and bloody rites which that superstition involved, but his own condition of slavery would, in all probability, have been continued and rendered permanent; for Big Chief and his men were numerous and powerful enough to have held their own against the Raratongans, while, at the same time, it was probable that he would have lost his master's regard, as he would certainly have lost his respect.

He could not help reflecting, also, how much the cause of Christianity must often suffer in consequence of the conduct of many seamen, calling themselves Christians, who visit the South-Sea Islands, and lead dissolute, abandoned lives while there. Some of these, he knew, brought this discredit on the name of Jesus thoughtlessly, and would, perhaps, be solemnised and sorry if they knew the terrible results of their conduct; while others, he also knew, cared nothing for Christianity, or for anything in the world except the gratification of their own selfish desires.

While he was yet pondering these things, Big Chief advanced towards him, and, taking him by the hand, led him into the centre of the concourse. To his great surprise and confusion the tall chief said—

"Now, Jowin will palaver to you. He is one Breetish tar—one Christian. He can tell us what we shall do."

Saying this, Big Chief sat down, and left Jarwin standing in the midst scratching his head, and looking with extreme perplexity at the vast sea of black faces and glittering eyes which were directed towards him.

"W'y, you know, old man, it ain't fair of you, this ain't," he said, addressing himself to Big Chief; "you've took me all aback, like a white squall. How d'ee s'pose that *I* can tell 'ee wot to do? I ain't a parson—no, not even a clerk, or a parish beadle!"

To this Big Chief vouchsafed no further reply than—"Palaver, you Breetish tar!"

"Wery good," exclaimed Jarwin, turning round, and looking full at his audience, while a bright smile lit up his sunburnt countenance, as if a sudden idea had occurred to him, "I'll do my best to palaver. Here goes, then, for a yarn."

Jarwin spoke, of course, in the native tongue, which we translate into his own language.

"Big Chief, small chiefs, and niggers in general," he began, with a wave of his right hand, "you've called on me for a speech. Good. I'm your man, I'm a 'Breetish tar,' as your great chief says truly— that's a fact; an' I'm a Christian—I *hope*. God knows, I've sometimes my own doubts as to that same; but the doubts ain't with reference to the Almighty; they're chiefly as regards myself. Howsever, to come to the point, you've gone and burnt your idols—"

"Ho!" exclaimed the whole assembly, with a degree of energy that made a deep impression on the sailor—just as one might be impressed when he has been permitted to become the happy medium of achieving some great end which he had never dreamed of being privileged to accomplish.

"Well, then," continued Jarwin, "*that* is a good thing, anyhow; for it's a disgrace to human natur', not to speak o' common-sense an' other things, to worship stocks an' stones, w'en the Bible *distinctly* tolls 'ee not to do it. You've done right in that matter; an' glad am I to hear from Big Chief that you intend, after this, to foller *the truth*. Old man, an' niggers," cried Jarwin, warming up, "to my mind, the highest thing that a man can dewot his-self to is, the follerin' out an' fallin' in with *the truth*. Just s'pose that chemists, an' ingineers, an' doctors was to foller lies! W'y, wot would come of it? Confoosion wus confounded. In coorse, therefore, they carefully *tries* to foller wots *true*—though I'm bound for to say they *do* git off the track now an' then. Well, if it's so with such like, it's much more so with religion. Wot then? W'y, stand by your colours, through thick an' thin. Hold on to the Bible! That's the watchword. That's your sheet-anchor—though you haven't seed one yet. It's good holdin' ground is the Bible—it's the *only* holdin' ground. 'How does I know that?' says you. Well, it ain't easy for me to give you an off-hand answer to that, any more than it is to give you an off-hand answer to a complicated question in the rule o' three. A parson could do it, no doubt, but the likes o' me can only show a sort o' reflected light like the moon; nevertheless, we may show a true light—though reflected. Chiefs an' niggers, there's asses in every generation (young asses chiefly) as thinks they've found out somethin' noo in regard to the Bible, an' then runs it down. An' them fellers grow old, an' sticks to their opinions; an' they think themselves wise, an' other people thinks 'em wise 'cause they're old, as if oldness made 'em wise! W'y are they asses? W'y, because they formed their opinions *early* in life, in opposition to men wot has studied these matters all through their lives. Havin' hoisted their colours, they nails 'em to the mast; an' there they are! They never goes at the investigation o' the subject as a man investigates mathematics, or navigation, or logarithms; so they're like a ship at sea without a chart. Niggers, no man can claim to be wise unless he can 'render a reason.' He *may* be, p'raps, but he can't *claim* to be. *I* believe the Bible's true because o' two facts. Fust of all, men of the highest intellec' have found it true, an tried it, an' practised its teachin's, an' rested their souls on it. In the second place, as the parsons say, *I* have tried it, an' found it true as fur as I've gone. I've sailed accordin to the chart, an' have struck on no rocks or shoals as yet. I've bin wery near it; but, thank God, I wasn't allowed to take the wrong course altogether, though I've got to confess that I wanted to, many a time. Now, wot does all this here come to?" demanded Jarwin, gazing round on his audience, who were intensely interested, though they did not understand much of what he said, "wot *does* it come to? W'y that, havin' wisely given up yer idols, an' taken to the true God, the next best thing you can do is to go off at once to Raratonga, an' git the best adwice you can from those wot are trained for to give it. I can't say no fairer than that, for, as to askin' adwice on religious matters from the likes o' me, w'y the thing's parfitly ridiklous!"

Jarwin sat down amid a murmur of applause. In a few minutes an old chief rose to reply. His words were to the effect that, although there was much in their white brother's speech beyond their understanding—which was not to be wondered at, considering that he was so learned, and they so ignorant—there was one part of it which he thoroughly agreed with, namely, that a party should be sent to Raratonga to inform the Cookee missionaries as to what had taken place, to ask advice, and to beg one of the Cookees to come and live permanently on their island, and teach them the Christian religion. Another chief followed with words and sentiments to much the same effect. Then Big Chief gave orders that the canoes for the deputation should be got ready without delay, and the meeting broke up with loud shouts and other pleasant demonstrations.

Matters having been thus satisfactorily arranged, Jarwin returned to his hut with a grateful heart, to meditate on the happy turn that had taken place in his prospects. Finding the hut not quite congenial to his frame of mind, and observing that the day was unusually fine, he resolved to ramble in the cool shades of a neighbouring wood.

"Come, Cuff, my doggie, you an' I shall go for a walk this fine day; we've much to think about an' talk over, d'ee see, which is best done in solitary places."

Need we say that Cuffy responded with intense enthusiasm to this invitation, and that his "spanker boom" became violently demonstrative as he followed his master into the wood.

Jarwin still wore, as we have said, his old canvas trousers, which had been patched and re-patched to such an extent with native cloth, that very little of the original fabric was visible. The same may be said of his old flannel shirt, to which he clung with affectionate regard long after it had ceased to be capable of clinging to him without patchwork strengthening. The remnants of his straw hat, also, had been carefully kept together, so that, with the exception of the paint on his face, which Big Chief insisted on his wearing, and the huge South-Sea club which he carried habitually for protection, he was still a fair specimen of a British tar.

Paroquets were chattering happily; rills were trickling down the hillsides; fruit and flower trees perfumed the air, and everything looked bright and beautiful—in pleasant accordance with the state of Jarwin's feelings—while the two friends wandered away through the woods in dreamy enjoyment of the past and present, and with hopeful anticipations in regard to the future. Jarwin said something to this effect to Cuffy, and put it to him seriously to admit the truth of what he said, which that wise dog did at once—if there be any truth in the old saying that "silence is consent."

After wandering for several hours, they came out of the wood at a part of the coast which lay several miles distant from Big Chief's village. Here, to his surprise and alarm, he discovered two war-canoes in the act of running on the beach. He drew back at once, and endeavoured to conceal himself, for he knew too well that this was a party from a distant island, the principal chief of which had threatened more than once to make an attack on Big Chief and his tribe. But Jarwin had been observed, and was immediately pursued and his retreat cut off by hundreds of yelling savages. Seeing this, he ran down to the beach, and, taking up a position on a narrow spit of sand, flourished his ponderous club and stood at bay. Cuffy placed himself close behind his master, and, glaring between his legs at the approaching savages, displayed all his teeth and snarled fiercely. One, who appeared to be a chief, ran straight at our hero, brandishing a club similar to his own. Jarwin had become by that time well practised in the use of his weapon; he evaded the blow dealt at him, and fetched the savage such a whack on the small of his back as he passed him, that he fell flat on the sand and lay there. Cuffy rushed at him and seized him by the throat, an act which induced another savage to launch a javelin at the dog. It grazed his back, cut it partly open, and sent him yelling into the woods. Meanwhile, Jarwin was surrounded, and, although he felled three or four of his assailants, was quickly overpowered by numbers, gagged, lashed tight to a pole, so that he could not move, and laid in the bottom of one of the war-canoes.

Even when in this sad plight the sturdy seaman did not lose heart, for he knew well that Cuffy being wounded and driven from his master's side, would run straight home to his master's hut, and that Big Chief would at once suspect, from the nature of the wound and the circumstance of the dog being alone, that it was necessary for him and his men-of-war to take the field; Jarwin, therefore, felt very hopeful that he should be speedily rescued. But such hopes were quickly dispelled when, after a noisy dispute on the beach, the savages, who owned the canoe in which he lay, suddenly re-embarked and pushed off to sea, leaving the other canoe and its crew on the beach.

Hour after hour passed, but the canoe-men did did not relax their efforts. Straight out to sea they went, and when the sun set, Big Chief's island had already sunk beneath the horizon.

Now, indeed, a species of wild despair filled the breast of the poor captive. To be thus seized, and doomed in all probability to perpetual bondage, when the cup of regained liberty had only just touched his lips, was very hard to bear. When he first fully realised his situation, he struggled fiercely to burst his bonds, but the men who had tied him knew how to do their work. He struggled vainly until he was exhausted. Then, looking up into the starry sky, his mind became gradually composed, and he had recourse to prayer. Slumber ere long sealed his eyes, setting him free in imagination, and he did not again waken until daylight was beginning to appear.

All that day he lay in the same position, without water or food, cramped by the cords that bound him, and almost driven mad by the heat of an unclouded sun. Still, onward went the canoe—propelled by men who appeared to require no rest. Night came again, and Jarwin—by that time nearly exhausted—fell into a troubled slumber. From this he was suddenly aroused by loud wild cries and shouts, as of men engaged in deadly conflict, and he became aware of the fact that the canoe in which he lay was attacked, for the warriors had thrown down their paddles and seized their clubs, and their feet trod now on his chest, now on his face, as they staggered to and fro. In a few minutes several dead and wounded men fell on him; then he became unconscious.

When John Jarwin's powers of observation returned, he found himself lying on his back in a neat little bed, with white cotton curtains, in a small, comfortably-furnished room, that reminded him powerfully of home! Cuffy lay on the counterpane, sound asleep, with his chin on his master's breast. At the bedside, with her back to him, sat a female, dressed in European clothes, and busy sewing.

"Surely it ain't bin all a long dream!" whispered Jarwin to himself.

Cuffy cocked his ears and head, and turned a furtive glance on his master's face, while his "spanker boom" rose with the evident intention to wag, if circumstances rendered it advisable; but circumstances had of late been rather perplexing to Cuffy. At the same time the female turned quickly round and revealed a brown, though pleasant, face. Simultaneously, a gigantic figure arose at his side and bent over him.

"You's bedder?" said the gigantic figure.

"Hallo! Big Chief! Wot's up, old feller?" exclaimed Jarwin.

"Hold you's tongue!" said Big Chief, sternly. "Go way," he added, to the female, who, with an acquiescent smile, left the room.

"Well, this *is* queer; an' I feels queer. Queery—wots the meanin' of it?" asked Jarwin.

"You's bin bad, Jowin," answered Big Chief, gravely, "wery bad. Dead a-most. Now, you's goin' to be bedder. Doctor say that—"

"Doctor!" exclaimed Jarwin in surprise, "*what* doctor?"

"Doctor of ship. Hims come ebbery day for to see you."

"Ship!" cried Jarwin, springing up in his bed and glaring at Big Chief in wonder.

"Lie down, you Christian Breetish tar," said the Chief, sternly, at the same time laying his large hand on the sailor's chest with a degree of force that rendered resistance useless. "Hold you's tongue an' listen. Doctor say you not for speak. Me tell you all about it.

"Fust place," continued Big Chief, "you's bin bad, konsikince of de blackguard's havin' jump on you's face an' stummick. But we give 'em awful lickin', Jowin—oh! smash um down right and left; got you out de canoe—dead, I think, but no, not jus' so. Bring you here—Raratonga. De Cookee missionary an' his wife not here; away in ship you sees im make. Native teecher here. Dat teecher's wife bin nurse you an' go away jus' now. Ship comes here for trade, bound for England. Ams got doctor. Doctor come see you, shake ums head; looks long time; say he put you 'all right.' Four week since dat. Now, you's hall right?"

The last words he uttered with much anxiety depicted on his countenance, for he had been so often deceived of late by Jarwin having occasional lucid intervals in the midst of his delirium, that his faith in him had been shaken.

"All right!" exclaimed Jarwin, "aye, right as a trivet. Bound for England, did 'ee say—the ship?"

Big Chief nodded and looked very sad. "You go home?" he asked, softly.

Jarwin was deeply touched, he seized the big man's hand, and, not being strong, failed to restrain a tear or two. Big Chief, being *very* strong—in feelings as well as in frame—burst into tears. Cuffy, being utterly incapable of making head or tail of it, gave vent to a prolonged, dismal howl, which changed to a bark and whine of satisfaction when his master laughed, patted him, and advised him not to be so free in the use of his "spanker boom!"

Four weeks later, and Jarwin, with Cuffy by his side, stood, "himself again," on the quarterdeck of the *Nancy* of Hull, while the "Yo, heave ho!" of the sailors rang an accompaniment to the clatter of the windlass as they weighed anchor, Big Chief held his hand and wept, and rubbed noses with him—to such an extent that the cabin boy said it was a perfect miracle that they had a scrap of nose left on their faces—and would not be consoled by the assurance that he, Jarwin, would certainly make another voyage to the South Seas, if he should be spared to do so, and occasion offered, for the express purpose of paying him a visit. At last he tore himself away, got into his canoe, and remained gazing in speechless sorrow after the homeward-bound vessel as she shook out her topsails to the breeze.

Despite his efforts, poor Jarwin was so visibly affected at parting from his kind old master, that the steward of the ship, a sympathetic man, was induced to offer him a glass of grog and a pipe. He accepted both, mechanically, still gazing with earnest looks at the fast-receding canoe.

Presently he raised the glass to his lips, and his nose became aware of the long-forgotten odour! The current of his thoughts was violently changed. He looked intently at the glass and then at the pipe.

"Drink," said the sympathetic steward, "and take a whiff. It'll do you good."

"Drink! whiff!" exclaimed Jarwin, while a dark frown gathered on his brow. "There, old Father Neptune," he cried, tossing the glass and pipe overboard, "*you* drink and whiff, if you choose; John Jarwin has done wi' drinkin' an' whiffin' for ever! Thanks to *you*, all the same, an' no offence meant," he added in a gentler tone, turning to the astonished steward, and patting him on the shoulder, "but if you had suffered all that I have suffered through bein' a slave to the glass and the pipe—when I *thought* I was no slave, mark you, an' would have larfed any one to scorn who'd said I wos—if you'd see'd me groanin', an yearnin', an' dreamin' of baccy an' grog, as I *have* done w'en I couldn't get neither of 'em for love or money—you wouldn't wonder that I ain't goin' to be such a born fool as to go an' sell myself over again!"

Turning quickly towards the shore, as if regretting that he should, for a moment, have appeared to forget his old friend, he pulled out his handkerchief and waved it over the side. Big Chief replied energetically with a scrap of native cloth—not having got the length of handkerchiefs at that time.

"Look at 'im, Cuff" exclaimed Jarwin, placing his dog on the bulwarks of the ship, "look at him, Cuff, and wag your 'spanker boom' to him, too—ay, that's right—for he's as kind-hearted a nigger as ever owned a Breetish tar for a slave."

He said no more, but continued to wave his handkerchief at intervals until the canoe seemed a mere speck on the horizon, and, after it was gone, he and his little dog continued to gaze sadly at the island, as it grew fainter and fainter, until it sank at last into the great bosom of the Pacific Ocean.

The next land seen by Jarwin and Cuffy was—the white cliffs of Old England!

Lightning Source UK Ltd.
Milton Keynes UK
UKHW011146180219
337528UK00001B/189/P